BIRTHDAY HEX

a novel

BIRTHDAY HEX

Copyright © 2021 Jennifer Rebecca

Cover Design and Formatting by
Alyssa Garcia

Editing and Proofreading by
Karin Enders

For more information about Jennifer and her books, visit:
www.jenniferrebeccaauthor.com

BIRTHDAY HEX

a novel

ACCIDENTAL HEX BOOK 1

USA TODAY BESTSELLING AUTHOR

JENNIFER REBECCA

ABOUT THE BOOK

When a fortune cookie on my birthday said, "you will meet a tall, dark stranger." I had laughed it off, but my mom wasn't so sure.

As a powerful witch she mixes potions like a professional chef, and casts incantations like a poet. And me? My greatest accomplishment is burning a can of soup.

A practical witch, I am not.

So when my dreams begin to piece together an ugly picture I'm not sure what to do or who to trust. And that tall, dark stranger turns out to be more than just a figment of my imagination.

This is more than a simple birthday hex . . .

For my mom, Vicki.
She is the best there is
And not once, in all my life, did she ever make me
feel less than.
Thank you for encouraging and inspiring me.
Thank you for being my champion.

PROLOGUE

Tall, dark & handsome

My breath saws in and out of my lungs and comes out of my mouth in little puffs. My heart is still beating wildly in my chest. A good orgasm will do that to you.

He stands up and leaves the bed where I lay sprawled on my belly, precisely where he left me when he was done with me. I blow my hair from my face in order to watch him go. His arms and back are nothing short of honed marble slabs of muscle and if that isn't fantastic enough, his ass and legs are works of art... no, they're works of the goddess. The tendons and muscles snap and flex in the most delicious way as he walks into the bathroom.

I hear the faucet run and watch as the light snaps off and then I get to watch the miracle that is *his naked front walking back toward me. His powerful thighs and magnificent cock, still semi-hard and thick and I let my eyes linger there before travelling up and up over his tight boxes of abs and broad chest with a light sprinkling of dark hair, and his beautiful smile surrounded by dark scruff and I can't help but think, "How is this my life?" How can this tall, dark and handsome man be mine?*

"Babe," he says, and his voice is deep and gruff. It fits him perfectly. I'm not paying attention to the words that he's saying, only his movements as he leans over me and in like he's going to kiss me. "Babe, it's time to get up."

That is unfortunate because I don't want to get up. I want to live in this bed as the boneless puddle he's made me to be and I want to stay here with my handsome lover until I die.

He leans closer and I know that his mouth is about to connect with mine and it's going to be sweet and tender and wet and powerful and everything because to this man, I am everything.

And then he places the pillow over my face until I can't breathe, until I can pull no air into my lungs, and everything goes black.

Beep... beep... beep...

I blink my eyes against the early morning light and reach for my alarm clock. I freeze with my hand over the button as it continues to blare because I realize that I'm not naked in the bed of a tall dark mystery lover who is trying to kill me, I'm dressed in flannel pajamas head to toe and in my own bed to boot.

But that's not what has the hair on the back of my neck rising.

What worries me the most is that I have never seen that man before in my life and this was more than just a dream. I don't know how I know it, but I just know that I know it. Then again, it could be the perspiration that slicks every inch of my skin or the throbbing ache between my legs.

But most of all, I know it was more by the residual burn left in my chest from where I fought to breathe.

This was a vision and a shitty one at that.

My mom is going to be so happy. Me on the other hand …

"Shit."

1

The Big 3-0

"I know a secret," Timmy, one of my most favorite kindergartners, says to me as he spots his dad in line to pick him up from school.

"Oh, yeah." I smile at him. Little kids are so funny. I love their enthusiasm for life. "What's that?"

"My daddy has a girlfriend, but he told me not to tell," he stage-whispers with an excited twinkle in his eye.

Well shit. This isn't what I thought he was going to say. Especially since this morning Timmy's mom told me there's another baby on the way and *not* that she and Timmy's dad are splitting up.

Shit on a shingle. This is one of those times that I would usually have a quick chat with Timmy to not repeat that and then side eye his dad but this afternoon I'm off my game. The betrayal of a lover so great that it leaves you dead will do that to you. Although, I'm not dead. I'm standing in the pick-up line at the elementary school that I teach at.

All day I fought the aftereffects of the dream—the vision—that's quickly turning into a nightmare. At first, I thought I needed to tell my mom right away. She's been a practicing witch for as long as I can remember and a good one at that.

Since my sixteenth birthday, she's been waiting for my powers to show their faces. Year after year there was just ... nothing. Never before had a witch's powers taken so long to come into play. Mom's devastated, but me? I'm used to it. I'm clumsy and klutzy. I'm awkward and a little weird. All great characteristics for a kindergarten teacher, but a powerful witch not so much.

The coven had started to prepare my mom for the actuality that I was a normie—that's a normal human for those not in the know—a mere mortal. I had even come to terms with it. So I should jump at the chance to tell her and everyone that I've had a vision, I finally have a power, something to show my ancestors that they didn't accidentally breed a timber wolf down to a chihuahua.

But as the day wore on, I wasn't so sure that my powers had magically manifested after over a decade of bupkis.

What if this vision is really a harbinger of things to come? And I don't mean the earth-shattering orgasm, for which I am long overdue, but my tragic and untimely death.

Now more than ever, I'm sure that I need to keep the vision to myself. The last thing I want is to scare my mom.

"Oh … that's … nice," I say awkwardly, choking on the words. And fuck me, I'm really off my game today.

A familiar dark blue BMW SUV pulls up to the front of the line and I feel like I can breathe a sigh of relief. Timmy's dad rolls down the passenger window and smiles at me.

"Hi, Penelope."

"Hi, Mr. Simmons," I reply as I pull open the rear door of the car for Timmy to climb in. I often invite parents to greet me more informally but there's always something about the way Todd Simmons says my name that feels more intimate than is appropriate. Even after redrawing boundaries, he still pushes.

"Bye, Ms. Jones!" Timmy shouts as he hops in his booster seat and pulls his seatbelt across his little body. "See you next week!"

"See you next week," I reply.

"And happy birthday!"

"It's your birthday?" Mr. Simmons asks, and I feel awkward that he knows this bit about me.

"Yes," I answer hesitantly. "The big 3-0."

"We should celebrate," he says, and I get the feeling that he doesn't mean me and the whole Simmons clan. I barely restrain my shudder.

"I have plans."

"Some other time then …" he lets his invitation for more hang between us, and I just let it trail off into the ether.

Even if his blond hair and blue eyes did it for me, he's still the married father of a student of mine and those are two solid lines that I won't cross. Ever. Not to mention, I may be about to be murdered by a lover so I'm a little hesitant to accept any invitation. Even to those not tall, broad shouldered, with dark hair, and haunting gray eyes.

I guess happy fucking birthday to me.

2

Fortune cookie say …

After leaving school, I barely make it to the restaurant in time to meet my mom for my annual birthday dinner at *The Happy Dragon*.

This is our spot, the place that Mom and I go when we have a hankering for Chinese food, and that hankering occurs often. At least once a week. And Mrs. Yee wouldn't have it any other way.

She and her late husband owned the duplex that my mom lives in, and they occupied the other half until he passed away in his sleep one night five years ago. Now it's just Mrs. Yee.

Mom, in her abundance of power over the natural elements keeps the communal garden of plants and herbs thriving while Mrs. Yee runs her restaurant empire.

"You're late," the older woman snaps from her spot by the front hostess stand.

"Little kid drama and creepy dads," I explain. "I could barely get away."

"You are the only girl I know who would be late to her own birthday party," she says excitedly and the white bob that she styles meticulously in place with a barrette at the side swishes wildly. She always makes me smile. She's like my other grandma since I never knew my father or his family. My maternal grandmother lovingly refers to him as my mother's sperm donor. "You'll probably be late to your own funeral."

That sentiment sobers me instantly. I really, really hope that my funeral isn't soon.

"Nah," I quip. "I'll probably just get lost on the way or get put in the wrong urn."

"I'd laugh but it's probably true," she says as she loops her arm with mine and leads me to the private dining room in the back of the restaurant that's reserved for special occasions.

Normally, Mom and I eat at an old battered wooden table in the kitchen. That's where family eats, Mrs. Yee always says. I used to do my homework there and she helped me nurse my first broken heart with an alarming ability to spoon ice cream into our bowls while nursing a serious grudge against the offending boy.

But birthdays are special. Always. Mom, me, Grandma, and Mrs. Yee. We celebrate in here and we do it big.

The walls are lined with silk tapestries painted in vibrant colors and depicting different scenes from old stories. I had heard Grandma refer to them as wards and enchantments more than once. Evil spirits can't reach the family here.

While Mrs. Yee is not a practicing witch like Mom and Grandma, she believes in the old ways that were taught to her by her mother, and her mother before her, and her mother before her, handed down over generations. When she met my mom, they formed an immediate kinship and they say that they understood each other instantly.

She pulls the heavy tapestry back for us to enter and my mom jumps up from the table and pulls me into her arms. "There's my baby!"

"Hey, Mom."

"Happy birthday, honey."

"Thanks."

My grandma, quieter and staider than Mom, pulls me into her embrace next. When she pulls back, she keeps me in her arms but looks at my face and in that moment, I know that she knows.

"Shh …" I plead and her eyes flare. She does not like secrets within the family, but I don't know what else to do.

"Everyone, sit down," Mrs. Yee says and shoos

us all to the round table that's laid with what seems like a million dishes. She's pulled out the stops for my big birthday and it makes my heart squeeze. I love these women so much.

"Thank you, Mrs. Yee," I say. "This must have taken hours."

"Birthdays are special," she says quietly. "The birthdays of my only granddaughter, even if not by blood, are more so."

Tears burn the back of my throat as I look around the table at the three most important people in my life. So I sit down and enjoy my birthday dinner.

We pass dishes of all kinds around the table and fill our plates as we fill the special room with love and laughter. I couldn't imagine a better way to spend my birthday than here.

Afterward, when all the dishes have been cleared away, each produces a small gift from under their seats.

"You guys know I don't need anything," I tell them with a smile on my face. "Thank you."

"She says she doesn't need anything," Mrs. Yee whispers conspiratorially to my grandma in her accented voice. Her English is near perfect. "But she lives in that awful apartment building on the other side of Queens."

"I can hear you." I laugh.

"I think you were meant to, darling girl," my

mom says drily. "Now, open mine."

She hands me a small velvet box and I carefully snap open the lid. Inside is a necklace, a pendant made of a small glass ball with a dandelion inside. Somehow, it seems to sparkle and shine as the light hits it but knowing my mother, there's more to it than that.

"Never forget to hope and wish," she whispers as she plucks the pendant from the box and slips the silver chain over my head.

"Thank you," I whisper.

"Mine next," Grandma says and hands me a pink bag with white tissue on top. I pull out another small box and snap it open. Little labradorite earrings glitter at me.

"Grandma ..."

"To connect the dots," she says with a knowing eye. "And for clarity of the mind."

"Thank you."

"There's more," she says, and I reach in the bag and pull out a lavender cardigan. "The one you're wearing is hideous."

"Thanks," I say with a laugh. If anything, she's honest.

"Now mine," Mrs. Yee says.

She hands me a small bag and I pull out three solid jade bracelets that must have cost a fortune. I've never seen anything so beautiful, and she slides the stack over my hand so they rest at my wrist.

"To keep you safe from harm," she whispers with her love for me shining in her eyes. "And to give you harmony in your heart and your soul."

"Thank you," I whisper.

"Now, cake!"

We all turn to the doorway that leads to the kitchen as her staff brings in a cake decorated with gorgeous wildflowers. This, I know, was my grandma. There is an artist's hand in everything she does.

They sing happy birthday and pass around huge pieces of cake which we all happily fall on like we're starving and not like we just ate a twelve-course meal. Because Grandma may decorate with an artist's hand but she bakes everything with love and an alchemist's soul. This confection is nothing less than perfect.

I tried to bake once upon a time but it turns out you can burn water. Who knew?

We sit and visit, talking about what's new in our lives and teasing each other, not like we don't see each other almost every day. Our lives are so intertwined, and we love it that way. Our bellies are beyond full and it's almost time to say goodnight.

"Now the fortune cookie," Mrs. Yee says as she passes a basket around. We've all been trained to know that you cannot hand someone a cookie, they have to choose their own fortune or else it won't come true. Although she has slapped my hand before with a terse, "Not that one."

I smile at the memory and close my eyes, reaching into the basket and let my fortune find me.

The wrapper crinkles as I peel it back and the crisp cookie makes a delicious snap as I crack it open. I don't look at the fortune until I've finished chewing the cookie as everyone else chooses their own cookie.

"Birthday girl first," Mom says as we start the family tradition of reading them aloud.

"Fortune cookie say you will meet a tall, dark stranger ..." I read to the room.

"Good," Mrs. Yee says. "Then maybe you will finally land a man."

"You do look like you could use a little ... stress relief." My mom laughs good naturedly. She's always been one to overshare.

"An omen," Grandma whispers and she's not wrong because I only read half of the fortune.

The other half says, *"... He is dangerous. Beware."*

An omen indeed. Well, damn.

3

I need

I gasp and twist the bed sheets in my hands as he spears me with his tongue. My legs draw up around his head on their own and he places his heavy hands on my thighs and pries them back open.

It's too much. And yet it's not enough in a way that I won't ever be complete again without him driving deep inside me and joining us as one.

"Please," I beg. For him to stop or for him to eat me alive, I don't know. Only he does.

He slips his tongue from my opening and I feel empty and wanting but he doesn't make me wait long. He parts me with his thumbs and opens his mouth over me, sucking the life from me while he flicks the tip of his tongue over my clit.

I let go of the sheets and drive my hands into his hair, holding him to me, desperate for more of what he can give me.

He pulls me deeper as only he can. It's like he pulls me under the waves, and I lose my breath completely as the air rushes out of my lungs and I shatter into a million beautiful pieces.

My heart races but I open my eyes and watch as he kneels between my thighs and places the tip of the condom wrapper in his mouth, tearing it open with his teeth. I hear the foil crinkle as he tosses it away—where, I don't know, because my eyes are riveted to the veins and tendons in his tanned forearms as he rolls the latex down his impressive cock.

My mouth waters. I want it. I want him. But I won't have to wait long because he grips my thigh in his hand while he braces himself on the other arm to wrap my leg high on his waist as he presses the blunt head of his cock to my opening and drives deep.

"Yes," I pant.

I hold on tight, his thrusts hard and fast as he sets a punishing rhythm that we both desperately need. He presses the pads of his fingers into my hips in a way that I know I'll wear his marks tomorrow. But it's the way he savagely plunges into me that lets me know I'll feel him there for days.

I feel another orgasm build within me and blaze through me like an out of control rocket. But it's not enough. I need more.

"That's it, baby," he purrs as he feels me clench around him, reaching, grasping for the climax that won't come.

"Please," I beg again. "I need ... "

"I know what you need," he rumbles as he lets go of my thigh and slides his hand between us so that he can finger my clit as he plunges in and out of me. It's exactly what I needed.

"Yes, yes, yes," I moan as a shudder rips through me. "I need you."

His thrusts become erratic as he drives me forward in my climax. The bed banging loudly against the wall as he does.

And then, I just let go.

He drives deep over and over and then like a chain reaction, he plants himself inside me as my orgasm rips his from him.

He slowly glides in and out of my body as we come down.

"Penelope," he whispers and when I open my eyes, I feel a chill in the room. The magic of our earlier lovemaking is gone, and his face is dead serious. "Penelope, I need your help."

I gasp as I come awake.

My dream lover is long gone, and the room has grown cold. But the worst part of all is that I'm alone.

At least this time, he didn't try to kill me.

4
Monday Morning Blues and the Color Red

"And what color is this, class?" I ask as I hold up a blue paint chip from the local home improvement store.

"Blue!" they shout in chorus.

"And what things are blue? Raise your hands, please," I say quickly when they all bounce in their seats on the sharing rug to answer at the same time. "Timmy?"

"The sky!"

"That's correct. Anyone else?" I ask. "Maya?"

"My chair!"

"You are absolutely right," I tell the sweet girl. "The chairs at our tables are blue. What else? Meg."

"Your sweater?" she answers, pointing to the

lavender cardigan my grandmother gave me for my birthday.

I sigh. We had it for a minute there and then the wheels came off the track.

"Not exactly," I say hesitantly.

"That's purple, stupid," someone in the back shouts."

"We do not call each other stupid," I scold. "Do you need a moment to collect your thoughts in the corner, Andy?"

"No, ma'am."

"Then please apologize to Meg."

He looks at his sneakers and wiggles around on his spot on the sharing rug. It never ceases to amaze me that these kids think they can wait me out on something … anything really.

"I'm waiting," I warn.

"I'm sorry, Meg."

"I'm sorry that I called you stupid, Meg," I correct him. "That wasn't very nice."

"I'm sorry that I called you stupid, Meg," he parrots. "That wasn't very nice."

"Thank you," I say gently with a smile knowing what it cost him to be corrected in front of the entire class. Unfortunately, he hasn't learned yet that calling Meg out in front of her peers cost her much more.

And they say shaping the minds of the future is easy … Time to redirect those future minds.

"And what color is this?" I ask, holding up another card, this time without looking at it.

"Red!" the shout together.

I look at the card and see a bright red square. It reminds me of that dirty Polish book-turned-movie series where the girl falls in love with her mafia kidnapper. And the ... ahem ... boat scene.

My dreams over the weekend could have rivaled the boat scene. That is, when my dream lover wasn't trying to kill me. Those visions were so hot, I almost hope I do meet my tall, dark stranger in the daylight hours. Almost. But not if he's going to kill me.

Even now, I'm feeling a little overheated for lack of a better word. I need some fresh air ASAP. Thankfully, before I can get a look at the clock, the bell for recess rings.

"Recess time, class," I call out as they line up in their order by the door. I pull open the heavy wooden door and lead them out into the hall and through the school to the playground where the other kindergarten classes are all spilling out over the play equipment and soft grass.

"How was your weekend?" my friend and fellow teacher, Amanda, asks me. "Who ... Never mind, I see it on your face."

"Is it that bad?"

"Looks like it was a doozy," she says.

"I haven't been sleeping well," I explain with

the understatement of the century. That's assuming most people don't dream of being murdered by a sex god.

"I got your class," she says. "You go get an extra cup of coffee in the teacher's lounge to ward away the Monday Blues."

"You are an angel from heaven," I tell her as I take off running.

"If you could just tell all of the single men of New York and the surrounding areas that, it'd be great," she says drolly and I laugh.

I feel like a criminal who has just escaped from prison as I push open the door to the faculty lounge and head straight for the coffee maker. I pop the lid on my lavender travel mug and set it aside before I place the cup under the spout of the coffee maker and drop a pod in the top. I close the lid and press the brew button.

My head starts to pound, and I rub my temples with my fingertips but it's not enough. I grab a plastic cup from the cupboard and hold it under the faucet as I twist the acrylic handle. But something happens as the water starts to flow. I see it, clear and cool as it pours from the spout and then I blink my eyes and I'm no longer in the teacher's lounge of PS626 in Queens.

I am naked and in a large bathtub. Steam from the water rises up and fills the room as the tub slowly fills around me. The sound of the water run-

21

ning relaxes me after a difficult night at home. The anger that fills me when I think about my husband and how he doesn't appreciate me anymore. All I ever wanted was for Rodney to love me. To want me. But I guess I was asking too much.

The door clicks as the knob turns from the outside and the door is pushed open. I wonder if maybe I've finally gotten through to Randall and he's decided to surprise me now, in the middle of the day.

But when the door opens completely, it doesn't reveal Randall, but someone else entirely. Someone who knows me more intimately than Randall. I'm sad that my husband doesn't want me like he used to but this one does, and I've decided to grab hold of the opportunity. Maybe this is my second chance at happiness.

"Hey," he says with a smile on his face.

"Hi," I reply. "I didn't expect to see you today."

"I just couldn't stay away," he says as he pulls his polo shirt up over his head and drops it to the counter.

"Is that so?" I ask as I snuggle down into the warm water, hoping he likes what he sees as much as I know he does.

"Absolutely." he drops to his knees next to the tub and reaches into the water with a strong hand, dropping it instantly between my spread thighs.

He toys with me, his fingers moving over me before thrusting two deep inside making me gasp.

"Mmm." I purr as he takes me higher but then, without warning, he withdraws his fingers from my core, and I snap my eyes open. "What are you doing?"

"I'm sorry, Sarah," he says as he pushes up to stand over me.

I move to cover my nudity with my hands but what I should have done was ward off an attack. Feeling humiliated that now not one, but two men in my life want nothing to do with me, I just want to curl up and hide.

I never see him coming.

Before I know it, his hand wraps around my neck and squeezes. I gasp for air and I'm sure confusion glitters in my eyes.

He doesn't seem confused at all as he pushes me under the water.

I pull and scratch at his hands and arms but it's no use. He won't let me go.

My lungs burn. I can't hold my breath any longer.

Bubbles pop from my mouth as the air rushes out and the water rushes in. And then I let go and everything just ... fades away into nothingness.

I gasp for air and drop the cup that has been overflowing down my hand and grip the edge of the sink until I get my balance. My knees feel like

Jell-O and I'm not sure how I'll stand on my own, but I also know that I have to because there are thirty-five little kids on the playground waiting for me.

I grab my coffee mug and snap the lid on, not because I still want this coffee but because everyone knows that it's mine and I don't want anyone to know that anything is amiss. I have a feeling that if I told anyone I was suddenly dreaming about my impending murder, although he didn't say my name. What did he call me? Sarah, I think. Now who the hell is Sarah?

It feels like my whole world has tipped upside down and I don't know which way is up. If anyone heard the thoughts goin on in my head, they would think that I had lost my mind, and honestly, maybe I have.

I race back out to the playground and Amanda gives me a weird look. I wonder how long I was gone. I take a quick peek at the apple watch on my wrist and see that it's only been ten minutes. I wonder what the look was about then? But I also don't have time to dwell on it because I see that Mom texted me while I was deep in my waking nightmare … or daydream … Whatever.

> MOM: Come home the minute you get done at school. It's urgent.
>
> ME: Okay.
>
> MOM: Sooner would be better.

ME: I can't do that, and you know it.

MOM: Okay but don't dilly dally.

ME: I won't. Love you, Mom.

MOM: I love you more.

I sip my coffee and think, maybe I should talk to my mom. She always has the answers. The man was the same one that I've been dreaming about for days now, the lover who worships me and then murders me. Talk about mixed messages. But the worst part is that as the dreams continue, I'm left with even fewer answers than before. Like, who is this man and why does he want me dead? I just don't know. I'm going to have to figure things out and fast before it's too late.

My coffee is lukewarm and black, neither is how I take it, but I don't care. I just watch my kids as they play and laugh. Kids have such a happy carefree aura around them. I wish I could let all of my dark thoughts go but I just can't. There are too many unanswered questions. And as they swirl around my brain, I can't help but wonder, *who the fuck is Sarah?*

5

Mama said there'd be days like this

By the time the last kid is loaded up in their parent's car and the last bus has left for the day, I'm a basket case. I've picked off all the polish from my nails and ripped the cuticles to the point that they bled on three, if not four, fingers. And it hurts, dammit.

But not as much as being drowned.

I race back to my classroom and straighten everything. I wipe the desks down because while adorable, small children are a certifiable breeding ground of bacteria. I stack the little chairs on top of the short tables so the floors can be vacuumed tonight. I re-sort the books the way that they should be and then make sure the paint and paste are all put up in the cabinet where the kids can't help themselves. That's a rookie mistake that you only make once.

And then I race out the door like my hair is on fire.

I don't go home to change my clothes or get something to eat. I drive straight to Mrs. Yee's duplex. I pull my car into the parking space around back in the small alley that runs behind the buildings, across the way from the neat rows of small backyards.

I smell the natural rawness of the earth and hear the swish of the leaves on the tree branches as they wave me home in the wind. To the untrained eye, it looks as if both yards are overgrown, allowed to run wild, and completely out of control but in truth, the magic of nature and Mom have only grown stronger together. She's at the helm here. If my mom is home, she's out here. This is where I will find her.

The latch on the gate clinks as I swing it open and slip through, before closing it behind me. It wouldn't do for a normie to see her practice her magic out in the open. Mrs. Yee and I do our best to protect her and her craft here, to shield her from the prying eyes of the outside world.

I almost miss her as I make my way through the labyrinth of steppingstones woven through the sanctuary. She's on her knees, huddled over a stack of cards—*tarot*—and she's barefoot in jeans and a t-shirt, unaware that the weather has turned cool.

How long has she been out here?

But before I can say anything, her head snaps up and her panicked eyes lock on mine. "Penelope," she cries out.

"Mom?" I ask, suddenly feeling unsure. I'm scared. I'm not afraid or embarrassed to admit it either but I just don't know what to do. *Can I lay these burdens at her feet?*

"Come here, please?" she says in a tone that I usually only hear when she's angry or disappointed with me. It's her mom-voice.

"Okay," I reply. "What's wrong?"

"You tell me," she says cryptically, and I know that I'm screwed.

"I don't understand," I answer as I step over to where she's still kneeling and crouch down beside her.

"I decided to do your monthly reading today," she says as she looks me over, and I know then that she knows.

"Well then … fuck."

"*Fuck* is right," she snaps. "Oh, my beautiful child, what have you done?"

"Nothing!" I plead like a guilty child. "I swear. I've done nothing but have dinner with you and Grandma and Mrs. Yee on my birthday. That was it. That was just after it all started. I swear."

"What started?" she asks me softly, her voice

gentle now.

"The dreams."

"Dreams?" she asks, and I can hear the excitement in her voice. She's … hopeful for me, and I just wish that they would go away.

My gifts have finally appeared and I'm ungrateful for them and the burden they bring with them. I can't help but feel guilty because I was happier without them.

"Since my party," I start hesitantly. "I've been dreaming of a man."

"A man?" she repeats with a wicked twinkle in her eye.

"Yes, a man, and no, not like that. Well … yes, like that because in the dreams he's my lover but in the dreams, he also murders me."

"What?" she gasps, her face falling. This is not what she was hoping for at all, and, honestly, neither was I.

"I'm murdered every time I go to sleep," I admit. "And it's been happening since Friday night."

"You had a vision?" she asks quietly.

"Of my death."

"But you had a vision …"

"I guess," I reply. "Truthfully, I don't know." I've been coasting on the fact that I was a shitty witch with no powers for thirty years now. I haven't exactly been studying.

"What else?" she asks me.

"That's it. There is nothing else," I answer before remembering why I came here today. "Well …"

"What?"

"Today I had a dream—"

"A vision," she corrects.

"Today I had a vision while I was filling a cup with water in the sink. One minute I was in the faculty lounge and the next I was naked and drowning in my bathtub."

"That explains a lot," she replies.

"Like what?" I ask quietly.

"Look at the cards," she says. "I only pulled three today."

I look down and wince. Wow, if ever there was a stack of bad cards she could have thrown, this was it. *Ten of Swords, The Tower,* and *The Devil.* Fuck me running, that is terrible.

"Yikes," Mom says when she looks at the shit show of cards that I've pulled.

"You could say that again," I mutter.

"Ten of Swords," she points out.

"Betrayal."

"Yes," she says softly. "Being murdered by a lover is definitely a betrayal."

"Agreed," I whisper.

"The Tower."

"Disaster or destruction," I whisper.

"That could also be you destroying illusions

or a breakthrough," she explains. "I was worried before, but now, knowing that your gift is one of sight, I'm not so sure."

"Mom, I'm pretty sure this is nothing but bad."

"Maybe," she says thoughtfully before moving on. "The Devil."

"I feel like that's self-explanatory," I drawl. "It's the devil."

"It could also mean pleasure," she says with a smirk on her face.

"Mom, I'm dreaming of being murdered by a lover," I remind her.

"Well, then maybe you'll get laid before you go on to the afterlife."

"I'm going to be betrayed by a silver-tongued devil with dark hair and a body to die for! This is not the time to give me shit about my sex life."

"You mean lack of. Honey, I have more of a sex life than you do."

"I don't want to know that!" I snap.

"Why not?" she asks. "You should be glad. With the right lifestyle and diet, you could be as active as I am when you're my age and enjoy it as much as I do."

"That's if I live that long," I say, rolling my eyes.

"Well, there is that."

"Mom—" I start.

"I'm just saying," she says, justifying her new

reasoning. Personally, I think I liked her better when she was freaking out as much as I am. "You did get that fortune from the cookie the other night. The one about the tall dark stranger."

Oh shit, she's right.

"Mom—" I try to interrupt her, but she's lost in the fantasy of me with a man who will give me good orgasms.

"What did it say again?" she muses. "You will meet a tall dark stranger. That's so romantic."

"Mom—"

"Mmm." She hums. "I think I want a tall dark stranger too."

"Dangerous."

"You always were so serious," she says, rolling her eyes just as I did moments ago. "Sex doesn't have to be dangerous. But a little wild might do you some good."

"Mom!" I shout.

"What?" She looks at me startled.

"I only told you half of the fortune," I explain. "It said 'You will meet a tall dark stranger and he will be dangerous.' I didn't think it was a big deal and I didn't want to worry you."

"You didn't want to worry me?" she screams. And dammit, why do I feel like I'm about to be grounded. I'm thirty years old, I can't be grounded. At least I hope not.

"Yes?"

"Well, let's go," she says, snapping her fingers. "We need to go to your apartment and get the fortune. I know you keep them."

I do. I keep every one. There was always something about the fortunes from cookies and how much belief Mrs. Yee put into them. It always felt a bit … magical. So I kept them. I have a huge glass jar on a bookshelf in my apartment. It's like a large cookie jar with a glass lid and when I saw it in the store, I knew exactly what I would do with it.

But the fortune that set this whole nightmare into motion isn't in my special jar on my bookcase with all of my favorite books and other treasures, it's in my purse. For some reason, I couldn't let it go and drop it into the abyss with all of the others.

I've kept it with me.

"Well?" she snaps.

"It's not at my house," I whisper.

"You threw it out?" she screams.

"No."

"Well, then where is it?"

"With me."

"Oh, fuck."

"Mom?" I ask. I'm terrified. I don't want to know. But at the same time, I have to.

"If your powers were coming in at the time that you chose that fortune," she begins. "And you felt strongly enough to keep it with you, then it's important."

"Fuck is right."

"Give it to me now," she says. "We have to throw the cards again so that we know what we're up against."

I race back to my car and dig through my bag. Shit! Now where is it? And then my fingers brush the slightly crumpled strip of paper and I snatch it out of the bottom of my bag. I turn and race back to the garden and drop to my knees next to my mom.

She takes the slip from my fingers and I feel the loss instantly. She closes her eyes and tips her head back to face the sky before touching the slip of paper to her forehead. Once she's focused, she places it in front of her and shuffles the cards before dealing the top three.

And my heart sinks.

Ten of Swords, The Tower, The Devil.

I'm so screwed.

"Mom—" I whisper.

"No!" she snaps. "You shuffle this time. Maybe it's me. You shuffle. You deal."

With a shaking hand, I shuffle the deck and focus. I flip over the top three cards and close my eyes. I don't want to see what I know is there.

Ten of Swords, The Tower, The Devil.

No.

"Do it again," she says. "Maybe you weren't focused enough."

I shuffle the cards three times and then flip the

top three cards over and I want to vomit.

Ten of Swords, The Tower, The Devil.

I feel a dull pounding behind my eyes. I feel sick. I feel defeated. I just want this day to be over.

"Try it one more time…" she says.

"Mom—"

"No," she says strongly. "We'll call your grandma. And Mrs. Yee. Everything will be all right. You just wait and see. We'll figure this all out."

I smile sadly. "I know."

"It'll be okay."

"Okay," I repeat. "I don't feel well. I think I need some rest."

"Okay. Make sure you drink your teas for balance and do your yoga before you lay down," she says, going full mom on me. "You know it helps."

"I do. I'll see you later, Mom."

"I love you."

"I love you more," I tell her.

"Impossible." she smiles.

I pick up my fortune, not wanting to be separated from it, and walk back through the garden and clank again through the hidden chain link gate that keeps her magical sanctuary safe. I climb into my car and drive to my apartment.

I don't make my tea that she mixes especially for me and I don't do yoga or meditate. I kick off my shoes and flop face down onto my bed.

Bogey, my cat, jumps up next to me with a loud

"meow!" and I stroke his soft fur.

It's then that I remember that I never told my mom about Sarah.

6

The all seeing google

Who is Sarah? Or Randall?

Nothing makes sense. Not one thing about this makes any sense. And if I'm being totally honest here, I'm scared. It scares me that I might be about to die. The feeling of being extinguished by someone close to me, someone that I love, is terrifying. Sure, I've never been overly lucky in love, or anything else for that matter, but still. No one's tried to kill me yet.

I strip off my clothes and toss them in the hamper. I pull on an old pair of sweatpants from a previous boyfriend and a tank top. I know it's ridiculous to keep someone's sweatpants but dammit, they're comfy. He took my virginity, so I felt it was only fair to keep his pants.

"Merow."

"Hey, Bogey," I coo to my sweet cat.

I'd been thinking of getting a cat about six months ago. My love life was looking bleak, and I was feeling pretty sorry for myself.

Amanda made fun of me when I wouldn't let her set me up with another one of her husband's loser friends. She said if I wasn't going to even try to date that I should just go adopt all of the cats and get started on my lonely life.

That hurt my feelings, I'll admit. I was even angry. But part of me wondered if it was a good idea. I didn't want to date just anyone. That was a waste of everyone's time, and I was getting to be of an age that I wasn't going to waste my time on someone that wasn't worthy of me.

That meant no more guys who called my ass fat or stole the last slice of pizza. No more guys who hooked up with girls at the gym because they thought they were God's gift. And definitely no more guys who pretended to forget their cash in the ATM so I would have to pick up the huge dinner bill for not only him and me, but also his friends.

I was done being a chump, but I wasn't done looking for my prince charming to ride along on his noble steed.

But I was lonely. And I do like cats. So I figured that the next day or even over the weekend, I would go to a local shelter and find a cat that might like me.

I was feeling pretty down so I ordered a pizza and picked it up on my way home. I'd just grabbed a plate and loaded it up with two huge pieces when there was a knock on my window. This would be normal if I lived on the ground floor, but I don't. I'm on the fifth.

I looked out the window and what did I see? But the most gorgeous black and white cat, pawing at the glass of my window. He must have climbed up the fire escape. I was terrified that he would slip and fall. Even a cat with nine lives left wouldn't make a fall from the fifth story so I quickly unlocked the window and slid the pane up.

"Merow," he said and trotted his way in with his big bushy tail like he'd been waiting for me for ages.

He climbed onto the sofa and settled in happily like he'd been doing it for ages. He lifted his head and blinked his big owl eyes at me in a "Well, what are you waiting for?" kind of a way.

So I grabbed a plate from the cupboard and filled it with pizza. Pizza that Bogey was all too happy to share. It turns out he likes sausage but loathes olives of any variety.

We settled onto the sofa and I picked up the remote from the coffee table and switched on the television. Casablanca came on and seeing as how it's one of my all-time favorite movies, I was happy to watch it. But when Humphrey Bogart came on the scene as Rick Blaine, my kitty squatter perked up.

"You like Bogart, do you?"

"Merow."

"Huh," I muttered. "How about that?"

We watched all of Casablanca and then the Maltese Falcon came on and I was in old movie heaven. Apparently so was my new kitty friend because he was into it, too.

When the movies were over and the pizza was put up, it was clear that he wasn't going anywhere. When I went to bed that night, I left the window over the fire escape cracked in case he wanted to go home.

The next morning, he was waiting for me.

I decided to call him Bogey after one of my favorite actors. I bought cat food and tuna on my way home from work. The next week when there was no sign of him leaving, I paid the pet deposit with my building and took him to the vet for a checkup.

Now, he's just mine. Or really, I'm his.

I order Chinese take-out on an app on my phone and then set it on the counter. I pull a half-full bottle of wine from the fridge and pull the cork. The glasses are never far away in a kitchen this small, so I pull one down from the cupboard and pour myself a pretty full glass. Not that I'm sure I should be mixing wine and ominous visions but at this particular juncture, I'm not sure it can do much more damage other than, you know, actually dying.

I drink my glass and then another while I wait for my dinner delivery. I can't seem to clear my mind. The man—my lover—was so familiar to me. I can't see how this is a story that I'm removed from when I feel his hands on my body and his lips on mine every time I close my eyes. And then I feel the water fill my lungs as he holds me under.

No matter how familiar he is to me in my dreams, I know that I've never met that man before in my life. I might know his face, but I don't know his name. And the fact that I have carnal knowledge of a man that I've never slept with and yet I still know that he's going to be the very end of me … I just can't wrap my mind around it.

The buzzer sounds. It's my Uber Eats delivery. I buzz him up and hand him cash including a decent tip and shut the door. I make my mu shu chicken into rolls of the soft pancakes and plum sauce on my plate. I make my way back over to the sofa and sit down with Bogey.

I pick at my dinner while feeding him bites of chicken and egg. He has a bowl of kitty kibble on a fancy mat in the kitchen but he still mooches off me every time. I try my best to relax but it's no use. I just can't. Images swirl around behind my eyes and I can no longer see the evening news, instead I see the stranger's smile just before he pushes me under.

But there's one thing I can't let go of, why did he call me Sarah? And who is Randall?

I can't take it anymore. I set my half-eaten dinner aside and pick up my laptop. There's something about the dream that has me wondering if it was me at all and not something that had already happened to someone else.

I need to consult the all-seeing eye of Google.

I look up "Sarah, Drowning" and get nothing. I look up "Sarah and Randall" and get a slew of baby and bridal registries. And then I look up "Sarah, bathtub, drowning, New York" and bam! There it is.

Sarah Cramer, wife of Police Lieutenant Randall Cramer, found dead in her bathtub. No foul play is suspected.

I read through the article and gasp. No foul play! That can't be true. Sarah was murdered by her lover. If it was Sarah who was murdered. The more I read, the more I'm sure that Sarah is who I've been dreaming about.

I look for more articles about her death and find an obituary that reads:

Sarah Elizabeth Cramer was born January 28, 1980 in Suffolk County, New York. She is a graduate of Suffolk High School where she met her hus-

band, Police Lieutenant Randall Cramer. They were married August 25, 2007. Preceded in death by her parents and grandparents, Sarah's only living family is her husband. She is remembered as a loving wife and friend.

Loving wife and friend. She was friendly, all right.

I think of the dream where she's naked and burning up the sheets with the tall, dark stranger and not her husband, Randall. That wasn't nice. I shouldn't be thinking that.

I just don't know what to do. Maybe I should call the police department. I take a quick look at the clock on the cable box as I reach for my phone. It's after ten. Only crazies call the police at this time of night. I'll call first thing in the morning, that's what I'll do.

With a plan to put into motion, I feel my appetite return. I carry my plate back to the kitchen and fill it up. I finish my dinner and clean up before heading to bed. I feel better knowing that maybe this will all be over with just one quick phone call in the morning.

Famous last words, right?

7
Bad dreams

"**S**arah!" my husband snaps.

"What?" I ask.

I wasn't paying attention. I was making my shopping list for when I head to the grocery store later. I should have been paying attention because when I look up into his face, still handsome even though he wears his years on it now, Randy is angry.

"Were you even listening?"

"Yes," I reply and flinch at his cold, hard gaze. It's hard to look at him like this. Once upon a time he loved me so much that it shone in his eyes, now there's nothing but disappointment. "No."

"I said we have an important dinner with the Mayor and the city attorney this weekend," he says.

I want to tell him no. I don't want to go to another stupid dinner with men who puff out their chests and pat each other on the back for a job well done. A job they didn't even do because they have all ascended the ladder so high that they no longer get their hands dirty and those duties fall on the backs of those below them.

But if I do go, I'll see him ... and that's a temptation too good to resist.

"Okay," I smile sweetly, and Randall narrows his eyes. "I'll make sure I pick up the dry cleaning while I'm out today."

"That would be great," he says as he continues to watch me carefully.

It's unnerving. I know that this is a fraction of the intensity that criminals got from him when he was working cases. I'm his wife, not a criminal and yet, I can't help but feel like he doesn't trust me anymore. And I guess he shouldn't, really.

"I'll be home late tonight," he says before he turns his back to me and walks out the door without a hug or a kiss or an I love you.

The truth of it all whispers over my skin as I stand alone in the brightly lit kitchen. This house that once felt so warm and inviting is now nothing but cold.

He knows ...

I gasp as I sit up in bed, clutching the covers to my chest. My heart is racing and sweat slicks my skin. When I was a little girl, I used to think that if I hid under the covers, the boogeyman couldn't get to me. How wrong I was. Now I know that not only is the boogeyman real, but if he's coming for you, you'll never be safe again.

Now, more than ever, I'm sure that Sarah played a dangerous game. Bored housewives often do even though the outcome is never what they had hoped for.

It's a tale as old as time and a reminder to myself that there are no happily ever afters. Sure, Mrs. Yee had Mr. Yee until he died but both my mother and grandmother were left to raise daughters alone.

Love is nothing but heartbreak and, in this case, it's deadly. This is more than just a little bad dream. This is a nightmare.

8

Dream man

By the end of the week, I'm dragging. Not only am I not sleeping well, but I'm anxious. It's like there's this impending doom that I can't get away from.

Amanda and I are working the pick-up line together. I have the kindergartners and first graders and she's at the other end of the line with the second and third graders. It seems like chaos, but it actually runs pretty smoothly. We do it every day so, once we get the kids and parents with the program, it goes pretty well.

Timmy holds my hand, bouncing on the balls of his little feet in his batman sneakers as a familiar dark blue SUV crawls its way through the pick-up line.

I have to hold my breath in my lungs as the car moves closer. I can only hope that it's Timmy's mother in the car instead of his father.

As I've evaded Mr. Simmons inappropriate advances, I've seen less and less of Mrs. Simmons and more and more of her wayward husband. I'm not actually sure what to do about it at this point.

"Hello, Penelope." Mr. Simmons greets me with a smile that makes the hair on the back of my neck stand on end. There's something about him that just makes me uncomfortable.

"Good afternoon, Mr. Simmons."

"You know I asked you to call me Paul," he says as he smiles even wider.

"Yes," I reply noncommittally as I help Timmy into his booster in the back.

"Do you have any plans tonight?" he asks, and I panic.

I need to make it clear that I am not an option for him. But what do I do? Thankfully, I don't have to because Amanda skips up to me and links her arm through mine.

"Ready to go?" she asks me breezily. "We don't want to be late."

"Late for what?" Mr. Simmons asks.

"Our double date," she lies easily. "Our boyfriends are coworkers. We're meeting them as soon as we leave here."

"Right," I add lamely. God, I suck at lying.

"I didn't know you had a boyfriend," he says. His face has lost some of its earlier humor.

"It's a new development," I reply and Amanda pinches me hard under my arm where he can't see her hand.

"Well, then," he says. "We'll let you get to it. Have a good weekend."

"You too," I reply. I shut the door, and he pulls away, wheels screeching.

"God he's such a creep," she says. "I don't know what his deal is with you. He needs to catch a hint."

"Is it that obvious?" I ask.

"That he's obsessed with you?"

"Yeah."

"Oh yeah," she says. "All the teachers and some of the PTA are talking about it."

"What?" I gasp.

"I mean, not everyone," she shrugs. "We don't talk in front of his wife. Did you what she's pregnant again?"

"Yeah," I say sadly.

"Well, now we need to go out," Amanda says as we walk back toward the classrooms. "We have to have a double date to get to."

"You do know that we don't actually have boyfriends, right?" I ask with a laugh.

"Then we better go out tonight to find some quickly," she winks.

We close up our classrooms for the weekend, stacking chairs on desks and books back where they go. When everything is as it should be, I grab my tote bag and my purse and meet Amanda in the hall as she locks up her classroom.

"Well, where are we finding these new boy-friends?" I ask with a smirk.

"At the bar," she answers with an eye roll. "Obviously."

"Obviously."

We pile our stuff in our cars and drive to the bar everyone goes to. It's a small hole in the wall. Nothing fancy, for sure.

As I pull my keys from the ignition and sling my bag over my shoulder, I can't help but wonder what the hell am I doing here? This isn't like me. I don't go to bars looking for men.

Men are nothing but trouble.

But before I can turn back, Amanda is there, standing next to my car with a smile on her pretty face.

Maybe I should do this. Maybe I should forget all about the devil and the tower. I need to have a night out where I can drink a beer and eat bar food. I need to laugh with a friend.

Music from an old jukebox plays in the corner. The room is filled with round wooden tables and chairs. At the back is a rectangular bar backed by mirrored shelves stacked with every bottle imaginable.

Amanda and I make our way to the bar and pull up some stools. I hang my purse on the hook under the bar, right by my knees, and settle in

"What'll it be, ladies?" the bartender asks with a broad smile as he makes his way down to us. He's young and blond and very handsome in an all-American kind of way.

"An IPA and a plate of nachos," Amanda asks, and suddenly that sounds like the best thing ever.

"I'll have the same," I answer with a smile.

"Coming right up." He pulls two bottles of beer from a cooler below the bar and pops the caps before placing them in front of us. "Food will be up in a bit."

"Thanks," we both reply.

We lapse into easy conversation about work and family. She's been at the school about as long as I have and lives with her parents after going through an unhappy divorce from her high school sweetheart. They never had kids. She says she's happy but I can tell his betrayal still hurts.

The bartender delivers our dinners and, as we eat, he begins to openly flirt with Amanda who is outwardly having none of it. But I can tell that she's secretly pleased by the attention and I think Nate, the bartender, can tell too.

I sip my beer and smile at their banter while hanging back to let them dance around each other without interruption. Nate leans further over the bar toward Amanda. I should get going and let them have their moment. I'll go home and call mom and then watch a movie with Bogey.

I reach to set my empty bottle on the bar top and excuse myself when a heavy hand gently falls to my back gaining my attention.

"Can I buy you another?" a man asks from beside me, and I find myself dumbstruck, not only by his beauty and sheer masculinity but by the icy light of interest and something more in his clear blue eyes.

The devil himself has come calling.

This is my dream man and I'm in real trouble.

The last thing I hear is the shattering of glass when the bottle slips through my fingers, missing the bar and hitting the floor.

Amanda calls my name, but I'm lost to the swirling abyss and everything goes black.

9

I won't hurt you

I blink my eyes open. I was having a wonderful dream where I was snuggled up in the arms of a man. It's been a long time since someone held me so tenderly and I'm enjoying it.

I've missed being cared for like this. Besides, I'm so tired and he's so comfy. Is it so wrong to want to sleep just a little while longer?

But when I open my eyes, I find the icy, yet warm stare of the man from my dreams looking down at me. *Oh God.*

I scramble. I try to get away, but he locks his arms tighter around me, holding me in his lap. He won't let me go and now I'm trapped in the arms of a cold-blooded killer.

"Brody, could you take Amanda to get some

water for Penny now that she's returned to the land of the living?" my dream man asks the man standing with my friend.

"Sure thing," he answers before turning to Amanda. "Let's go, sweet cheeks."

She shoots me a worried glance before scurrying out the door behind him. I'm worried too. She just left me alone in a back room of a bar with a cold-blooded killer.

"I won't hurt you," he says, but his voice is all wrong. It's much deeper, rougher than the one that has haunted my dreams for days now. It startles me for a moment and then I get my senses back.

"I don't know that at all," I whisper and then my eyes go wide. What in the world would possess me to tell a killer that I don't trust him? Maybe I really am about to die.

"Whatever you think you know, I can promise you that you don't," he says in a low voice.

"I don't know anything," I say quietly.

"Don't lie to me," he warns, and I open my mouth to protest his factual accusation when the door opens.

Amanda comes through the office door with a large glass of water in her hands. Brody follows in on her heels with a look of apology for not distracting my friend longer.

"Thank you," I say as I take the glass in my hands and sip it all while wondering just who this is holding me in his arms. And his friend who's content to let him do it.

"What happened?" Amanda asks. "Are you all right?"

"I think so," I reply. "I must be more tired than I realized."

"You did have a long week," she adds. "What with your weird moment in the faculty lounge and all."

"What accident?" my dream man asks.

"It was nothing."

"It wasn't nothing," Amanda disagrees. "Not to mention Mr. Simmons." She shudders.

I shoot her a glare, imploring her to close her mouth but it doesn't work. Some days I wish I was a real witch and not a normie and I could do things like make her stop.

"Who's Mr. Simmons?"

"No one."

"Doesn't sound like no one to me," he says, his voice low in a warning.

"Doesn't sound like nothing to me either," his friend says from across the room with a huge smile on his face.

"Who are you?" I ask them, narrowing my eyes on the friend.

"Detective Brody Adams, NYPD," he answers with a huge smile. "And you?"

"No one that would garner NYPD attention," I

answer. "I'm not that exciting."

"I wouldn't bet the ranch on that," my dream man says. I turn my head and look up at him. "I'm Detective Hunter Buchannon, NYPD."

"Of course you are," I snap. "Can I go now?"

"No," he says, frowning at me.

"Why not?"

"I need to make sure you're all right first," he answers.

"Sure you do," I mumble to myself, rolling my eyes and he grips me a little tighter. I need to remember to guard my tongue around this man. I know that I can't trust him. "Well, I think I need to go home and rest."

"That's probably a good idea," Amanda agrees. "We'll go out again some other time. We still have to find some decent fake date candidates."

"Well look no further, ladies," Brody says. "Hunt and I would be glad to be your dates, fake or real. Right, Hunt?"

"Yeah."

"I'll see you to your car," Brody says to Amanda, distracting her. "Then I can get your number."

"Oh, okay," she says before turning to me. "Are you going to be okay?"

I look at her face, there's a glimmer of excitement in her eyes. She wants to walk out with Brody, and I don't blame her. He's good looking, charming, has a decent job. That's the holy grail as long as he's not married or an axe murderer.

Can I let her go? Can I let her leave me with a man I don't know and don't trust? One who I think murdered his lover?

"Great! Call me tomorrow," she says before I have a chance to answer and turns to let Brody lead her away. Awesome.

Once the door closes behind them, I hold my breath while the devil, who has me in his arms, looks me over. It feels like he sees everything, like I can't hide anything from him. There will be few little secrets going forward.

Isn't anything sacred anymore? Apparently not.

"You know you're safe with me," he says quietly, his handsome face made up of strong, masculine features, so close to my own. When did he move in?

I don't have the words to give him. I don't trust him. The truth is, I know him to be a murderer. I'm not safe with him, I'm clasped tightly in the jaws of a lion. One I can't voice my true thoughts to, or he'll crush me. So I just nod.

He stands and for the first time, I realize just how tall and strong he is. He slowly lowers me, letting me slither down his body until my feet touch the floor.

I blink my eyes dazedly and look up at him. I take in his long legs encased in fitted worn denim with a little bit of fraying at the edge of the pocket and up, up, up over his flat belly and his broad shoulders until I look at his face. He's keeping it open for me. This is the look on a face that says, "Trust me!" and I know that it's probably nothing more than an act. The thought sends a pang through my heart.

"Let's get you home," he says as his eyes burn me.

"I'm okay," I reply quietly, hoping that he'll let me go and I'll never see him again. "You don't need to go out of your way."

"It's no trouble," he says, a knowing smile spreading wide across his face. The flash of bright white teeth against his tanned skin and dark scruff is shocking. "Besides, we have some things to talk about that are better said in private."

I wince. That can't be good. Anything that has to be said in private is most likely very deadly. I sigh. I guess this is it. Too bad I don't have my mom or my grandma's skills. Then maybe I'd have a fighting chance to protect myself but other than a few recent nightmares that might be visions, I'm still just a normie.

"Ready to go?"

"As ready as I'll ever be."

"It'll be okay," he says. "I promise."

And then he leads me from the small back office of the bar out past my car and to a dark SUV. It looks like something the president would ride in.

He beeps the locks and pulls open the passenger door for me.

I eye it dubiously but when he just raises one lone eyebrow, I know that there's no chance for escape. I climb in and buckle my seatbelt as he shuts the door behind me.

He walks around the vehicle and climbs in, buckling his seatbelt quickly and keying the ignition. He pulls out of the parking lot and heads toward my apartment building.

I shouldn't be surprised that Detective Buchannon knows exactly where I live.

It's too much to hope that he had no idea who I was and happening upon me was just a coincidence. Although there's nothing coincidental about drowning your lover so that her husband doesn't find out about you.

He pulls up to my building and somehow manages to get there right as a car is leaving a curbside space right in front. How does he do that? That never happens to me.

Now I'm irritated. How dare this man bring me to my home to kill me in private and get a primo parking spot. Can't he leave me some dignity to die with? I guess not.

He pulls his keys from the ignition and unbuckles his seatbelt before pushing open the driver door and stepping down.

I should have run. I should have jumped from

the vehicle and run screaming through the night like a crazy person, only I didn't.

Instead, I just sit here in stunned silence as Detective Buchannon prowls around the car like a predator.

I'm out of time and out of luck. I'm going to have to think fast if I'm going to get myself out of this mess.

He pulls open my door and holds out a hand for me like a gentleman. To anyone passing by on the street, it would look like he's returning me home after a date. Like maybe he'll walk me up and kiss me at the door before saying goodnight, or even stay until morning. The truth is, this is anything but.

I reach across my body and press the release button on my seat belt. It springs free with an ominous click. I let it retract across my body and then place my shaky hand in his upturned palm and let him pull me from the SUV.

When my feet hit the pavement, he closes the door behind me and hits the lock button on his key fob before pocketing his keys. He leads me through the door to my building. We take the stairs and I feel like I'm dragging my feet.

Is this what it feels like to be walking the green mile? I can't help but feel like any moment someone will clang a tin cup against the bars in my imaginations and yell "Shawshank!"

By the time we reach the door to my apartment, I'm a nervous wreck. We stand there and stand there, staring at the door and nothing happens. I think I might be sick. I think I might pass out.

"Babe, you gonna unlock the door or are we gonna stand out here all night?" he asks me, and I remember I'm the one with the keys.

Excuse me for being a little distracted by my impending murder.

"Oh, right," I mutter as I slide my bag off my shoulder and start digging through it for my keys. I feel them at the very bottom and pull them out. I'm shaking so bad I can barely get the key to the lock.

Detective Buchannon sweeps them from my hands and nimbly inserts the key into the lock, the tumblers rolling over with an audible click. And then he pushes the door open.

I choke back my fear and take a step inside. And then another and another. I freeze when I hear the door close softly behind me and the lock flip, keeping me inside with Detective Buchannon.

I don't turn around to look at him, I just face straight ahead, hoping that he'll make it quick. He doesn't seem like the kind of guy to make me suffer so at least there's that.

My breath saws in and out of my lungs and I still feel like I'm not getting enough oxygen. Black spots dance about the corners of my eyes.

"For fuck's sake, Penelope!" he roars. "I'm not

going to kill you!"

"What?" I gasp and spin around only to see that he's right behind me. "W-what did you say?"

"I'm not going to kill you," he repeats.

"Then what do you want with me?"

He watches me for a moment before he seems to come to some conclusion. What that is, I don't know. I'm not even sure he's going to impart that knowledge on me until he opens his mouth and answers. "I need to find a killer and I think you're the key."

"M-m-me?" I stutter. "I don't know any murderers. "What makes you think that I do?"

He just watches me.

I wonder if this is how he gets criminals to cave when he interrogates them. Does he just stare at them until they can't stand it anymore?

"Brody?" I gasp, coming to the wrong conclusion. "He has Amanda! We have to go get them!"

"It's not Brody," he snaps. "And would you stop moving dammit?"

I stop my movements and realize that in my panic, I must have begun pacing. "Sorry."

"Think," he says. "Think really hard about why I might think you would be the key?"

I blink.

He couldn't possibly know. Even Amanda doesn't know. And if he did, he wouldn't believe me. The only logical conclusion is he knows that

I know that he's the killer and wants me to admit it first. He wants to toy with me like a cat with a mouse trapped in its paws. But I won't go down without a fight and I won't die on my knees either.

"Where do you think you're going?" he says low.

"Uh …"

I slowly start backing up into the kitchen. I need a weapon. Or a distraction. I need to escape. I need to get to my mom. She'll know what to do. She has the skills and the talent to protect me. I shouldn't have thought to go it alone. I should have heeded her advice.

And then I remember the amulet around my neck. I've worn it every day since my birthday. Something told me that I would need it and I need it now. I grab the small glass orb and pull, snapping the chain. I toss the whole thing to the floor, when it smashes, the magic held within will swirl up and fill the room, providing me with protection.

Only that does not happen. The glass amulet hits the floor with a quiet *tink* and then rolls under the sofa.

"Oh hell," I mutter.

"You should know an amulet like that will only work to protect you from evil. I'm not that, babe," he says quietly.

"I don't know that!" I snap. "I don't know anything so just leave me alone."

"I can't do that, Penelope."

"Why not?"

"You know why."

"I don't know anything," I cry. "I swear it!"

"You're different," he says. "You know it and so do I."

"No," I gasp.

He can't. There's no way he can know. I'm a normie. These visions are just an anomaly.

"Yes," he says. "I know who you are. What you are—"

"No."

"I can sense it," he says.

"I'm normal," I whisper, and he steps closer, into my personal space, and pulls me into his arms.

"Honey, you are anything but," he says.

I think he's going to kiss me—it looks like he's going to kiss me—and I'm so lost in his ice blue eyes that I even want him to. But then he doesn't, and I can't help but feel a little ... disappointed.

"Detective Buchannon?" I call his name hesitantly.

"I think it's probably time you call me Hunter," he says gently.

"Why?"

He watches me, willing me to know something that I don't. Only when it becomes abundantly clear that I am totally clueless, he lets out a frustrated breath. It's the tiniest of sighs but I hear it. Besides, we're standing so close together, his breath, tinted with cinnamon, wafts across my lips.

"That's not for now," he says. "Now, you just need to know that we're going to be spending a lot of time together."

"But why?" I ask, my frustration growing by the minute. Why won't he just answer me?

He flashes me a smile. It's a slash of white in his tanned face. "Because I like you, Penelope. And besides, I need your help.

10

I need you

The silk sheets are soft and cool against my heated skin. I lay back on the pillows and watch as Hunter moves toward me, his clothes do nothing to hide the power of his body. His covered form is juxtaposed to my completely naked one.

I slowly lift my arm and beckon him to me. His eyes heat at the invitation and I watch as he strips his clothes off one piece at a time and lets them float to the floor.

"Come to me," I whisper as I hold my arms out to him.

"Penelope," he growls as he kneels on the bed.

"I need you," I tell him. I let my legs fall open as he moves over me, covering me with his body. I

cradle his hips with mine and feel the hard length of him at the very center of me as he twines his fingers through mine.

"I need you, too," he replies, his eyes penetrating mine and it's so much more. This connection, it's everything. We are one.

"Hunter." I'm overwhelmed with the feeling that we were made solely for each other as he slides deep inside of me, connecting us in the deepest of ways.

"No!" I scream as I come awake with a start. "No."

I can't be connected to Hunter Buchannon. He can't be mine. I cannot be the other half to a man who terrifies me.

Just as the cards said, he's the devil himself. Fate can't be that cruel. The very piece of me that's been missing this whole time, the one that my soul calls out for can't be a murderer.

Maybe I'm destined to carry on the Jones family curse after all …

Beep … beep … beeep …

I blindly reach for my alarm clock where it sits

on my nightstand and miss. Dammit! It clatters to the floor while still shrieking louder and louder. I force my eyes open and reach for the blaring alarm clock where it sits nestled in the plush carpet. As soon as I clutch it in my fingers, I switch it off and drop it back on the side table and let out a groan.

After my red-hot dream turned into a steaming nightmare, I couldn't get back to sleep. I tossed and turned for hours. No matter what I tried—meditation, yoga, walking around my apartment, warm milk, counting sheep—nothing worked. I couldn't stop the rising tide of anxiety that was swirling through my system, knowing that the one the universe had sent just for me, was a cold blooded killer.

And if that wasn't enough to make me cry, there was the hungry ache between my legs that refused to go away.

As much as I don't want Hunter Buchannon, I want him. I'm determined to put the deadly detective out of my mind. All I need to do is stay away from him. That shouldn't be too hard.

It turns out it's going to be hard as hell.

After I stumbled into the shower and then pounded a pot of coffee, I dressed in my customary teacher gear of an A-line sundress with a denim jacket over it and t-strap sandals. I grabbed my tote bag and headed downstairs only to remember that my car is still at the bar after my Sleeping Beauty routine.

"Damn," I mutter to myself before digging my phone out of my purse to call up an Uber. Just as I open the app a dark SUV pulls up and I feel my blood pressure start to climb because I know exactly who is behind those tinted windows.

"I figured you'd need a ride this morning," Hunter says. "So I had Brody ask Amanda what time you have to be at the school."

"Thanks," I reply quietly.

"Hop on in."

I quietly let out a frustrated breath and pull open the passenger door. I climb in and pull the door shut behind me before setting my bag on the floor in front of me. I pull my seat belt across my body and when I lean in to click the buckle in place, his scent surrounds me, heating my blood. I press my thighs together, hoping to make the ache go away.

One look at Hunter from the corner of my eye and I can see his lips pull in an annoyingly handsome smirk. That fucker knows exactly how he makes me feel.

I stay silent and keep my gaze trained on the road in front of us. I ignore him even though I'm painfully aware of his presence near me. When he finally pulls up in front of the elementary school that I work at I let out a relieved breath and I swear I hear him chuckle. But when I look at him, his face is nothing but a noncommittal poker face.

"So I'll pick you up at six," he says and I snap my head back around to look at him.

"What did you say?"

"That I'll pick you up for dinner at six," he replies.

"I don't remember agreeing to a date."

"I asked you to dinner, not a date," he says with a sexy smirk on his full lips. "But I'm happy to accommodate whatever you'd like."

"No thank you."

"Dinner it is then."

"What? No," I splutter. The first warning bell rings. I need to get to my class to greet the kids but I'm here, arguing with a man who I am, without a doubt, attracted to and who may or may not be a murderer. It's too much. I can't compute. I think my brain is about to explode.

"Too late," he says. "We agreed."

"I didn't agree to anything," I say as the bell rings.

"You better run, or you'll be late," he says, and I think I hate him.

I let out a little growl of frustration under my breath.

He shouldn't have heard it and yet, I know he does by the chuckle that rumbles up from his chest as I slam the door and walk away.

I barely make it to my classroom before the first kids arrive for the day. I have them sit on the circle rug and look at a book while I pull the chairs down from the tables and get everything arranged for the day. I feel out of sorts. Not just because of the visions of a murder, but because of Hunter.

I didn't want to be alone anymore, but this is just … I don't know, a lot.

He's a lot to take in even if he's not a killer.

I have a strong feeling that, in the best-case scenario, I'll get my heart irrevocably broken.

Worst case scenario, I'll get unalive.

I don't like it. I don't like it at all.

"He was such a good kisser," Amanda says dream-ily while I nervously pick at my sandwich at lunch. "So, of course, I'm going to see him again tonight."

"Of course," I parrot.

"Are you going out with Hunter?" she asks.

"I don't know," I answer. I do. I know without a doubt he's going to show up at my apartment to-night at six to take me to dinner but I'm not ready to admit it yet. He scares me and I'm not sure what to do with that.

"What's there not to know?" she asks. "I saw the way he was looking at you last night."

That draws my attention and I snap my head up—away from my turkey and avocado on whole wheat—to look at her. "What way was he looking at me?"

"Like a feral dog with a juicy steak within reach," she says, and I feel my heart rate spike.

"I don't think he looked at me like that …" I hedge.

"Honey, anyone who saw you two together last night got laid," she says.

"Amanda!" I admonish and quickly look around to see if anyone else heard her. Thankfully, they didn't.

"What?" she laughs. "It's true. Even I got an orgasm out of it, and we didn't actually do the deed."

"Do the deed?" I ask. "You just met him last night."

"True, but I couldn't help myself. There's just something about him," she says. "And besides, I never figured you as one to slut shame."

"What?" I gasp. "No, never. I would never judge you. It's just that those men make me nervous and I don't know why."

She mulls over my words for a moment before nodding her head and swallowing a bite of her apple. "Actually, I can see that."

"You can?"

"Yeah," she says, crunching up another bite. "Brody and Hunter are men like you've never met before."

"How's that?" I ask. "I've met plenty of men."

"But not men like them," she answers. "When God made them, He broke the mold. Those men are alpha males. They can't easily be pushed away or put off by you. Those are men who know what they want and take it and you don't know how to react to it."

It's true. I don't know what to do. "So how do I get him to move on?" I ask and she laughs. "What?"

"Oh honey, you don't get a man like that to move on."

"Well then what am I supposed to do?" I ask, frustration filling my tone.

"You hold on and enjoy the ride."

11
Whatever you do, don't run

*A*fter my illuminating conversation with Amanda, I decide that I won't be anywhere near my apartment by six o'clock this evening. Is it the mature decision? No. Is it even a smart one to be toying with a man like Hunter Buchannon? Also, no. That doesn't mean I'm not going to run like a big chicken. I am. I'm just going to run to my mom. She will have all of the answers.

I close up my classroom as soon as the last kid is gone for the day and pull my tote bag out of the bottom drawer of my desk. I don't have car rider pick up duty today and thank God for that because I'm not sure I could handle it if I did.

Mr. Simmons would home in on my weaknesses and I'd be flat on my back in the back seat of his fancy SUV before I could blink. I really wish someone would tell Mrs. Simmons what a creep he is. I'm just thankful I don't have to deal with him today.

I walk a block away from the school and then hail a cab in front of a Bodega that Amanda and I grab sandwiches and waters at for lunch often.

Ten minutes later, he's pulling up in front of my mom's house. She's standing on the front stoop of her side of the duplex, just waiting. I smile. She always knows when I need her and there she is. She's the best mom a girl could ask for.

I slip some cash through the partition for the cabbie and race up the steps.

Mom wraps me in her arms and ushers me inside. "I had a feeling you were coming," she says. "What's wrong, baby?"

"Everything," I whisper.

"You met your devil," she surmises. Of course she would remember the ominous reading she gave me not too long ago.

"That and so much more, Mom."

"Come sit down and I'll make you some tea," she says.

I follow her through the downstairs of the house to the kitchen at the back, overlooking her garden. She fills a tea kettle with water and prepares me a mug with a baggie of herbs she grows and dries herself. The fragrant smell goes a long way to relax me and reminds me of my childhood.

The whistle on the kettle blows and she pours the steaming water over the tea bag and hands the mug to me. "There you go. Let that steep a bit while you tell me what's going on."

"Oh, Mom," I tell her. "It's all a mess."

"No mess can't be cleaned up," she says. "We just have to start at the beginning. Tell me everything and we'll see what we can't figure out together."

I do. I tell her how my dreams have turned erotic and star the man I met last night; the one who insisted on taking me to dinner tonight even though I've made it clear he scares me. I tell her what Amanda said about him and everything else. And I feel like a huge weight has been lifted off of my shoulders because I'm no longer shouldering this burden alone. It's always been Mom and me against the world and this is no different. I never should have kept any of it from her.

"Well that is all quite overwhelming," she says. "No wonder you seem out of sorts. I think you need to go outside and ground yourself to nature for a bit. I'll call Grandma and Mrs. Yee and we'll have ourselves a little witchy woman powwow," she says with a laugh.

"That sounds good," I tell her. "Thanks, Mom."

"Of course, darling. I'll do anything for you.

We all will."

"I know."

I drink the last of my tea and rinse out my mug in the sink before kicking off my sandals and shrugging free of my jacket. I push open the screen door and step outside. I feel the rough concrete steps under my feet as they take me down into the garden.

The second I feel the grass and dirt under my heels I close my eyes and take a deep breath. I spread my arms out wide and tip my head back to feel the late afternoon sun on my face. I smell the dirt and the sunshine and feel mother nature all around me, grounding me to the here and now. My anxiety finally begins to drift away.

I don't open my eyes when I hear the screen door swing open on its squeaky hinge behind me. I know it's my mom or my grandma or Mrs. Yee. Only people who love me and protect me are welcome here tonight. I am safe.

"Well, everyone is on their way," Mom says. She's quiet for a moment and I wonder if she hasn't gone back inside but I also didn't hear the back door slam closed again. "You know, I knew there was something different about you, but I couldn't put my finger on it until right now."

"What's that, Mom?" I ask.

"The mating fever."

"The what?" I ask and my eyes fly open as I turn to look at where she's standing in the doorway watching me.

"The mating fever," she answers. "You've come in contact with your mate and he's ready to claim you. You're ready to be claimed. It's why you feel frantic. The energy of the claim is coursing through you now."

"What?" I gasp. "You can't be serious."

"I wouldn't have believed it myself," she says. "Although, that young man over there does lend proof to the obvious."

"What?" I gasp as my head snaps around and my eyes lock with those of none other than Detective Hunter Buchannon.

"You ran from me, Penelope," he says, his voice a low rumble as he steps out from between the trees to my left.

"No," I whisper. I look from him to the right where the gate that leads out of my mother's yard stands open and inviting.

"You were supposed to meet me at six," he warns.

"No," I say as my heart beats faster and faster. "I didn't promise you anything."

"Oh, this is a surprise," I hear my grandma say from behind me. But I can't look at her, I can't take my eyes off of the threat Hunter presents as he looms off to my left.

"We agreed," he growls. "And you ran."

"No," I whisper.

"I know!" my mom says excitedly. "What fun!"

What the hell are they talking about? Fun? I think not. How about terrifying? This man could be a killer and even if he's not, he still scares the daylights out of me.

He takes another step toward me and I know that I have to go. I can't stay here. The gate is looming in the distance. I can make it. I know I can.

"Penelope?" my mom calls out as I've already made my decision.

I'm turning back toward the gate. "Yeah?"

"Whatever you do, don't run."

"Sure, Mom," I say, but I don't mean it. We all know I'm lying. I take off, digging into the ground to push myself away as far and as fast as I can go.

I make it to the gate and push through it. My breath saws out of my lungs as I push on through to the alley that runs behind the houses. I make it past one house and hear footsteps pounding behind me.

He's gaining on me, but I can't let him. I have to run. I don't know why but I know that I have to, so I push even harder.

I look around and there's no real place to hide. I'm not going to make it. I want to cry but I know that I can't give up. And then I'm grabbed around the waist and slammed back against the detached garage on the other side of the alley.

Hunter leans into me, holding me up against the garage. His hips pin mine in place and I feel the hard, thick length of him against my center.

The feel of him makes my breath catch in my throat and my nipples bead underneath my clothing.

Hunter seems to see it all and his eyes darken as his pupils take over in his own arousal.

"You shouldn't have run from me, Penelope," he warns and then he slants his head and crushes his mouth to mine.

I let out a whimper as he thrusts his tongue into my mouth, and I suck it deep. He kisses me hungrily, angrily, as he takes me. I grip his shoulder, digging my nails into him to hold tight as I rock my hips against him. The feel of his hard length between my legs pushes me higher and higher.

He shoves the skirt of my dress up around my hips and rips my panties from my body before stuffing them in the pocket of his jeans. He slides his fingertips through my folds and groans.

"Fucking soaked."

I whimper at his touch. I want more, so much more, but he takes his hand away from where I need it most, where I need him most. And then it's a rush of movement as his belt clangs between us as he undoes his jeans. I feel him, the blunt tip of his cock at my center but only for a moment and then he's driving up into me.

I wrap my legs around his hips, desperate to anchor him to me as he drives up into me over and over, pistoning in and out. My back scrapes against the side of the garage where he has me pinned but I don't care. I couldn't care if I tried to about anything other than his thick cock or the way that Hunter rides me against the wall.

"Yes," I pant and tip my head back against the building as he plunges in and out, driving me closer and closer to my orgasm and I want it like I want my next breath.

"Fuck yes," he rumbles as he traces his nose up the column of my neck, leaning over me.

He spears his fingers through my hair and tips my head to the side and pulls the collar of my dress down to expose my shoulder to his kiss. The way I cling to him and the wall behind me are the only things keeping me upright.

He holds me open and exposed to him as he spears me with his thick cock. I'm so close and yet, something is missing. I feel the whispered magic of a climax between two bodies but it's just out of my reach. I chase it down, squeezing him deep inside of me as I rock my hips to his rhythm.

And then something seems to break free inside him.

"You're mine, Penelope."

"Yes," I pant and let's be real, at this moment, I'd agree to just about anything.

"By the moon and the stars, I claim you as mine," he says.

Wait. What?

His voice has taken on a different tone. It's something more than lust, it's elemental but before I can ask, he tightens his grip on my hair. He pulls my head to the side just before he sinks his teeth into the muscles and tendons where my shoulder connects just below my neck.

It's the last bit I needed to send my climax careening through my body like a flash of white lightning. It burns so hot and so bright and then everything goes black.

12
Welcome to the Family

I blink my eyes open as my heart beats loudly in my ears.

Hunter's large frame envelopes me but where his hold before was rough, a primal possession, now it's sweet and tender. Gentle, even.

He has his face tucked into the crook of my neck, the very place that he bared and bit. But that can't be, can it? It feels like it was a dream, but I know that it's not because I can still feel him hot and hard inside of me, connected in the most intimate of ways.

He must feel me slowly coming back to the here and now because he raises his face to look me over. There's a new light in his eyes, a new understanding of one another and yet I can't help but feel like he knows all the answers to the test and I never studied.

I open my mouth, what I'm going to say, I don't know yet. Some things have to be handled on the fly. Like letting the guy you think is a murderer fuck you up against a garage in your mother's neighborhood. And the walk of shame aftermath that's soon to follow.

But his body stiffens under my hands, and he turns his head around to snarl at something behind him while shielding my body from an enemy I can't see.

"Well that escalated quickly," my Grandma says, and I feel my face burn with embarrassment to be caught like this.

"Don't be embarrassed, Penelope," she says. "Even the mightiest witches fall to the mate fate has chosen for them."

"True dat," my mom says.

"Oh my goddess," I groan.

"What's happening?" Hunter asks me.

"That's my mom and grandma," I answer.

"Time to meet the family I guess."

"You don't have to," I tell him, and he gives me a weird look. It's a mix of angry and if I had to guess, a little hurt too.

"Of course I do," he replies. "It's not every day I get caught in an alley with my pants down."

"We'll just meet you two back at the house,"

Mom says, a smile in her voice. As she turns away, she mutters, "Lucky girl."

Once they're gone, Hunter slides out of me and I feel empty, like part of me is missing. I unhook my legs from his waist and drop them down to the ground. The asphalt is warm and rough beneath my bare feet.

"Did that just happen?" I ask.

"I'm afraid so."

"Can I have my panties back?" I ask as he tucks himself back into his jeans.

"No."

"But," I whisper, embarrassed. "I'm … leaking."

"I know." He smirks.

"Fine," I snap before heading back toward my mom's house. "You're a real savage, you know that?"

"Something like that," he replies, and I can hear the smile in his voice.

Fine. Great. Whatever, even. I'll go do this walk of shame and then get rid of the murderer so that I can go back to my quiet life with my cat.

I don't need a man; I have a cat who is actually pretty demanding. He hogs the covers at night and steals all of the sausage off the pizza. Now that I think about it, I don't have room for another male in my life, especially one who is a murderer.

I push back through the gate and walk through

my mother's garden all while Hunter follows close-ly behind me. Apparently, he has no issue with his own walk of shame.

I pull open the screen door and see that my hu-miliation has no limits today. Sitting around the kitchen table is my entire family: Mom, Grandma, and Mrs. Yee, who smiles unrepentantly at Hunter as he walks through the door behind me.

"Is his ass as good as your mother said it was?" Mrs. Yee asks me in her slightly accented tone.

I want to crawl into a hole and die. I was also raised to never lie so I look her in the eye and tell the truth. "Yes."

Hunter throws his head back and laughs. It's deep and sexy and fills the whole room. No woman in a thirty-mile radius wouldn't want her last act on earth to be to make this man laugh like that again, including every woman in this very room.

He settles down only to see that we're all star-ing at him with open fascination.

I'm looking like a fish with my mouth hanging open. Mom winks at me, her eyes sparkling with mirth.

Grandma is studying us both. What she sees I don't know, only that she sees everything and misses nothing.

Mrs. Yee is still smiling like we bought her a Chippendale's dancer for her birthday, which inci-dentally we did two years ago, and she said it was the best birthday she ever had.

"Welcome to the family," Grandma says once everyone is quiet.

"What?" I gasp.

"I'm sure you two will want time to settle in together," Mom says. "The door here is always open."

"Now just a minute—" I start.

"We also like to have family dinner together on Sunday nights," Mrs. Yee says. "I cook."

"But—"

"That's true," Mom adds. "She's a fantastic cook. Have you ever eaten at Golden Dragon?"

"Yes," Hunter answers. "My partner, Brody, and I eat there once a week."

"I thought you looked familiar," Mrs. Yee says.

"Guys—" I try to wade in again.

"You're the good-looking policeman," she says. "You have the partner with the dimples."

"Yes," he answers. "I'll tell him you remember him."

"Now, you and Penelope go have fun," Mom says. "Enjoy the mating fever."

"Wait!" I shout.

"What?" Mom asks.

"He's not my anything," I shout and a warning growl sounds from behind me but I ignore it.

"Honey, he's your mate," Mom says.

"He can't be my anything because he's a murderer!" I shout.

"What?" everyone including Hunter shouts at the same time.

"You a murderer?" Mrs. Yee asks.

"Yes," I answer. "He's the one I've been dreaming about."

"So you have been having visions?" Hunter asks.

"Nooooo."

"Yes," he disagrees. "And I'm not a fucking murderer."

"You're not?" I ask.

"No. The victim was my boss's wife," he says. "He asked me to look into it. Brody and I are investigating it on the DL because we suspect someone close to the lieutenant killed his wife."

"Huh …" I mutter. "But I've been dreaming of you."

"Because you're my mate," he explains.

"But in my dreams, you kill me."

"I can see how that would cause some confusion," he bites out.

"Are you … mad at me?" I ask.

"Well, yeah."

"Why?"

Because you keep denying that you're my mate and it's starting to chafe," he says.

"But I don't even know you," I tell him.

"It doesn't matter because my soul knows you."

"That's crazy!"

"It is how it is," he explains. "The magic within you knows the magic in me."

"But I have no magic," I try to explain. "I'm normal."

"Oh baby," Mom says. "You are anything but normal."

"That does not sound good," I mutter. "You're magic? Like them?" I ask as I nod my head toward my family.

"No," he says gently. "Not like them."

"Of course not," Mrs. Yee says bluntly. "He's a wolf."

"What?" I gasp and he smiles flashing a set of blinding white teeth.

"I knew you looked familiar," Grandma says. "You're one of Hamish's boys?"

"Yes," he smiles. "He was my grandfather."

"He was a good man."

"That he was."

"Your cousin is in charge now?" she asks.

"Caulder," he answers. "He runs the pack up north now."

"That's right …" Grandma says before eyeing me and deciding she shouldn't speak in front of me like I'm a child.

"Oh, don't hold back on my account," I bite out.

"Penelope, don't talk to your grandmother like

that," my mom admonishes me.

"No," I say holding out my hand to keep everyone away from me. "This is not okay. I am not okay."

"I can see this was a lot to take in," my mom says, but I'm done.

I need to be alone. I need time to think, to clear my head, to scream or cry, I don't know. I just know that I can't do what I need here. And the worst part of it is, I can tell that they're all holding something back. This isn't even all of it.

"This is way past 'a lot to take in,' Mom." I sigh. "I have to go. I'll call you when I'm ready."

"You don't mean that, honey," she says sadly.

"I do."

"Penelope," Hunter says as I move toward the door. He reaches for my arm, but I jerk my body back as if he's burned me. A wounded look crosses his face that pangs around in my chest.

"No," I whisper. "Not now." I don't have time for this. I have to go. And then I push through the door and make my way down the concrete steps.

The grass crunches underneath my feet as I push through to the gate. I loop around the block, not pausing to let myself feel anything when I pass the spot by the garage where Hunter caught me. Instead, I walk further down the road to the bus stop.

The driver opens the doors and I climb the steps. As I pass, I hand him my money for the fare and find my way to an empty seat, never once noticing that I did this all without shoes on my feet. I don't feel anything at all, I'm numb.

I ride the few blocks to my apartment building where I thank the bus driver before the doors close behind me. After letting myself into my apartment, I drop my bag on the table by the front door and pour some fresh kibble in the bowl for Bogey, who look unimpressed with his meal.

I pull my dress overhead and pull on a tank and a pair of sweatpants before laying down in my bed. I pull the covers up high around my neck and settle in. The spot on my shoulder where he bit me is starting to throb in time with my heartbeat.

Everything about the last twenty-four hours is so messed up. I don't even know where to begin. Hunter claimed me, he owned my body and something far deeper and more precious. And the worst part of all is that I gave it to him.

It's when I hear the faint howl of a wolf in the distance that the first tear falls. And then another. And another.

Nothing is okay. I'm not okay.

I cry and cry letting the overwhelming feelings of being alone envelope me like a blanket, one that does not comfort. Then I drift off to sleep where I am nothing at all.

13

Bad juju

I think we can all agree here, that with my luck and recent questionable foray into the non-normie sphere of magic that I should abstain from this particular chapter. Consider it a great time to make some popcorn or get a glass of water ... or wine ... whatever. We don't judge here.

Just ... proceed with caution. I'd hate to blow up your microwave with some bad juju.

14
Monsters in the dark

The door clicks as the knob turns from the outside and the door is pushed open. Hunter prowls into the room with eyes only for me. Maybe he's my chance at happiness after all ...

"Hey," he says with a smile on his face.

"Hi," I reply. "I didn't expect to see you to-day."

"I just couldn't stay away," he says as he pulls his polo shirt up over his head and drops it to the counter.

"Is that so?" I ask as I snuggle down into the warm water, hoping he likes what he sees as much as I know he does.

"Absolutely." he drops to his knees next to the

tub and reaches into the water with a strong hand, dropping it instantly between my spread thighs.

He toys with me, his fingers moving over me before thrusting two deep inside, making me gasp.

"Mmm," I purr as he takes me higher but then, without warning, he withdraws his fingers from my core, and I snap my eyes open. "What are you doing?"

"I'm sorry, Sarah," he says as he pushes up to stand over me.

I move to cover my nudity with my hands but what I should have done was ward off an attack. Feeling humiliated that now not one, but two men in my life want nothing to do with me, I just want to curl up and hide.

I never see him coming.

Before I know it, his hand wraps around my neck and squeezes. I gasp for air and I'm sure confusion glitters in my eyes. He doesn't seem confused at all as he pushes me under the water.

I pull and scratch at his hands and arms but it's no use. He won't let me go.

My lungs burn. I can't hold my breath any longer.

Bubbles pop out of my mouth as the air rushes out and the water rushes in. And then I let go and everything jus t... fades away into nothingness.

The last thing I hear as the world goes dark is his deep voice saying, "Witches aren't the only monsters in the dark."

I gasp as I come awake with a start. A thick sheen of sweat covers my entire body and the room is spinning. Hunter says that he's not a murderer but still, my visions keep him front and center in the role. One way or another, he's going to lead me to my demise.

I push myself up from the bed and make my way into the bathroom. I turn the handles on the faucet and let the tap run. I splash cool water onto my face but it does little to wash away the cobwebs away from my brain or the hurt from my heart.

I cup my hands under the tap and drink the water down but it burns like acid in my stomach. I don't know what to do other than go back to bed and try and get some sleep.

The sheets stick to my clammy skin and they feel like heavy arms holding me down. I can't get away—from my bedding or the dangerous man who wants in my life. I know that this isn't the last I've seen of him. Hunter Buchannon has decided that I belong to him and he's not going anywhere.

I toss and turn for what feels like hours before finally falling back to sleep only to have my alarm go off what feels like mere moments later. There's a huge part of me that wants to pull the covers back over my head and hide from the world. Maybe if I never leave this apartment again, then I won't have to admit what happened yesterday.

I can't believe I acted that way. That wasn't me, not the real me, anyway. I live a quiet, albeit, lonely life. I love my family and my students. Bogey and I are content in our life together. Truthfully, he's a great cat.

I'm not the kind of woman who meets a tall, dark stranger in a bar and less than twenty-four hours later, lets him take her against the exterior wall of a garage. No matter what any fortune cookie would have you to believe.

The best I can hope for is that it was all a dream. A dream where dangerous men don't pursue quiet schoolteachers into relationships or sex or whatever the hell he wants which is probably a combination of everything including help finding a murderer ... or hiding one. Because, without a doubt, my dreams are telling me that I can't trust him, even if the aching in my body is saying to hell with it all because I want him above all else.

"Umpf." The air is forced from my lungs as the weight of my feline friend lands on my chest. We really should cut back on the pepperoni and sausage.

"Merow," Bogey says into my face.

"You're right, of course," I agree as I scratch him under his chin. "It's time to get up and face the day. Even if it's going to get me killed."

"Meow." If cats could roll their eyes, he would have. He's clearly over my dramatics.

"What?" I ask, solidly not ready to give up on my drama. "You'll live a great life with Mom when I'm dead."

"Merow," he rumbles as he hops off my chest and heads to the kitchen. I guess there's no time for my maudlin thoughts when his belly isn't fully topped off.

With a heavy sigh, I throw the covers back and climb from the safety of my bed. I pad into the kitchen and fill his bowl with a little tuna from the open container in the fridge. Bogey growls a bit when I don't give him more and I place the rubber lid that seals the can back up on it and pop it back into the fridge.

I drop a travel mug under the coffee maker and pop in a coffee pod. Whoever invented the Keurig is my hero. Nothing used to make me feel lonelier than brewing a whole pot of coffee for one. I let that heat up and brew while I take a quick shower.

I dry my hair and swipe a little light makeup across my face before pulling on jeans and a pretty floral blouse. I slide my feet into a pair of ballet flats before donning my armor. I slide the jade bracelets up my arm and slip the chain from my mother's amulet over my head. They give me the boost of confidence that I sorely need.

I make my way back into the kitchen where Bogey is nowhere to be found now. I pour some flavored creamer in my coffee and screw on the lid and grab my phone from the counter. I notice there are a ton of missed calls and text messages from a number that's not saved into my phone.

> 929-555-2010: Penelope, please call me.

> 929-555-2010: Baby, please call.

> 929-555-2010: Honey it's Hunter. I need to talk to you.

> 929-555-2010: Baby, I know you're freaked, it scared me too, but we gotta talk about this.

Uhh ... no buddy, we don't.

I don't want to talk to him. Actually, my new life plan is to avoid him at all costs. I do decide to save his number in my phone, so I know it's him when he calls again. I move my thumbs over the screen and type *Garage Fucker* ... then delete it. That's a little rude, besides, what if one of my kids sees it. That would be horrific. I type *Hunter* in with a heart emoji and then delete it because what am I twelve? Finally, I type in *Detective Buchannon* and leave it at that.

I toss my phone in my big tote bag before slinging it over my shoulder and heading out into the hall. I lock my door behind me and make the walk to where my car is parked, side-eyeing the front spot where Hunter found parking the other day.

I hit traffic from an accident, and it adds time to my commute. I barely make it through the front gate by the time the bell rings. It feels as if the whole universe is conspiring against me.

One thing I know for sure, I need to stay the hell away from Hunter Buchannon. He's bad news.

15
Unavoidable

"**D**id you kiss that boy, Miss Jones?" Emily, one of my students asks when she raises her hand during circle time."

"Uhh …" I start and feel like maybe I'm having a stroke. Thirty is too young for a stroke, right?

"I saw you in that boys truck outside," she says while I stand there making fish faces, completely robbed of the ability to speak by a four year old.

"Of course she kissed him, dummy," another student answers. "He's a policeman. He has a badge and a gun. I saws it when he got out of his truck to wave to her bye only she didn't see it on account of how she was running so fast. Why was you running anyways, Miss Jones?"

"The gun was pretty cool," Timmy adds.

"Guns are not cool," I interrupt them. "They are dangerous and even deadly if handled inappropriately. Right, class?"

I'm answered with a chorus of "Yes Miss Jones."

"But you did kiss him, right?" Emily asks and man, that kid is like a dog with a bone.

"Of course she did, dummy."

"Kids—"

"I'm not a dummy. You're a dummy."

"Kids—" I try again but am cut off by the bell for recess, Thank you God. "Line up and we'll head out to recess."

The kids throw up a cheer for recess that could have a lesser woman doubting their abilities to shape the minds of the future. Fortunately, the Goddess saw fit to bless me with more confidence than my actual ability should allow me to carry. Real talk: I burn soup in the microwave, a leader in the witchcraft community, I am not.

I hold in my sigh as I pull open the door to our classroom and lead them down the hall. We follow a class of first graders out onto the blacktop lined with four square courts and handball walls. My class scatters like ants at a picnic and I watch some of them join others and form lines to play Red Rover.

I'm lost in my thoughts this morning. Everything swirls around as I try to focus on the kids but all I can think about is Hunter and the woman he murdered. Everything about him begs me to trust him and yet, my dreams tell me otherwise. I just don't know what to do, other than avoid him at all costs. There's just no other solution and I'm not willing to die.

I'm lost in my maudlin thoughts when Amanda pops up beside me. She exudes happiness and sexual satisfaction. The afterglow is practically rolling off of her in waves, and I kind of want to punch her.

"Hey!" she practically sings like a goddamn Disney princess. "Isn't today a great day?"

I take in the smog and overcast skies and wonder how she decided this was beautiful. Like what kind of grading scale is she using? Is this how she grades her students? Not that there's much to grade on in kindergarten other than do they know their name or their colors and do they eat the paste? There are more paste eaters than you'd think.

"Yeah, it's great."

"I know," she breathes. Of course she'd fall in love with the murderer's best friend after two nights of wild monkey sex.

Shit. I'm being a bitch. I don't like being a bitch, period. It's not who I am. And I definitely do not want to be a bitch to Amanda. She's my best friend. My sister from another mister. My ride or die. She's the peanut butter to my jelly. I don't want to shit on her parade.

In my dreams, Hunter is the murderer, never Brody. If she's fallen in love with Brody, I'm going to support her and I'm sure that I can do that while avoiding Hunter like the clap.

"So … Brody, huh?" I ask as we lean back against the fence and watch our kids play on the playground.

"Yeah," she smiles broadly. "He's great."

"I'm glad," I smile back and this time, I mean it.

"So …" she starts. "You and Hunter?"

"Well," I reply. "That one's a little more complicated."

"How so?" she asks tipping her blonde head to the side. "He's your mate, right?"

"How do you know about that?" I ask. "I mean what… uhh… what makes you say that?"

"Well … Brody told me after he… Gosh, it felt like he *claimed me*. It was amazing, right? Like so much… I don't know, *more*."

"Yeah," I say and feel a pit open in my stomach. "It was amazing."

"Then what's the problem?" she asks. "It's okay, honey. I know. Brody told me everything."

Everything? I seriously doubt that. How can I tell her that I think he's a murderer? That the man my soul is tied to is a cold-blooded killer? I can't do that … or can I?

Amanda is my best friend. She's never given me any indication that I can't trust her and yet, I never let her fully in. She doesn't know about my family or our history.

"Can I tell you something and you promise not to freak out or tell anyone?" I ask.

"Of course," she says but then bites her lip nervously.

"What?"

"Well … I can't promise not to tell Brody."

I think about it. Does it really matter if she's going to share what I tell her with Brody or not? It stands to reason that Brody is a wolf like Hunter and if that's the case, he knows Hunter's secret, but does he know mine?

I could guess that Brody knows more about my family history than Amanda does and if the truth ever came to light from someone other than me, she'd be really hurt. It's probably best that I come clean now and deal with the fallout, even if she is going to be really hurt. At this juncture it's unavoidable.

"I can understand and respect that," I tell her before I take a deep breath and begin. "You have to understand that what I'm about to tell you you can't tell anyone. Okay?"

"Of course," she replies. "But you're scaring me a little."

"It's not scary, I promise you," I tell her but

then feel the need to back track a little. "Well …
most of it's not scary. I think I better start at the
beginning."

"Please."

"I come from a family of witches," I begin.
"One of the oldest living lines here in America and
powerful too."

"Why didn't you ever say anything?" she asks.

I flinch at the pain that she wears on her face
plain as day. "Because I was a normie."

"A what?" she asks.

"A normie," I explain. "Someone who comes
from witches but has no skills or powers."

"But you said that your family was powerful
…" she says as she tips her head to the side, trying
to understand me.

"They are," I try to explain. "but I wasn't."

"You weren't? So now you are?" she asks.

"Exactly," I answer. "Well … sort of. I'm not
powerful."

"Then what are you?"

"A disaster." I sigh. "I'm a bit of a mess."

"Come on. It can't be that bad."

"It is." With a heavy sigh I lay it all out on the
table. "On the night of my thirtieth birthday I started having nightmares of a lover who murders me."

"Jesus, that's terrible," she says.

"I know but that's not the worst of it. Earlier
that night we were having dinner at Mrs. Yee's res-

taurant and my fortune said 'You will meet a tall, dark stranger. And he will be dangerous.'"

"Oooh, nice. I bet that's Hunter!" she claps her hands excitedly.

"Don't get too excited," I warn.

"Why not?" she asks. "This is a sign that he's your mate. At least I think so."

"Maybe he is but that's not so good either."

"Why's that?" she asks me.

"We'll get to that in a minute," I answer. "But first Hunter is the lover that I dream murders me over and over every night."

"What?" she gasps. "He would never hurt you. He's meant to protect you."

"I don't know—" I hedge.

"Brody says it's a gift from the Goddess when she grants you a mate. That she's the other half of your very soul and without her, you're incomplete. He says it's their duty to cherish and protect their mates. And further their bloodlines."

Bloodlines? Oh fuck.

The sudden images of Hunter taking me up against the side of the garage flash through my brain on a loop over and over again and the one thing I notice above all else is the lack of a condom procured from his wallet.

Did he flip my dress up? Check.

Did he rip my panties off of me? Check, check.

Did he roll on a condom? Fuck no.

I'm so screwed. I count back the days in my head and hope to the Goddess that I'm not wrong. Although math never was my strong suit.

"Penny?" she calls quietly.

"What?"

"I lost you for a minute," she explains. "You just drifted away."

"I'm sorry. I think my life is spinning out of control."

"You said Hunter being the man in your nightmares isn't the worst of it …"

"No," I whisper. "The Jones curse is."

"What curse?"

"Any woman from my line will fall in love," I answer.

"Well that doesn't sound like a curse."

"She'll be so happy in love and have a baby that she thinks will unite them, a girl, it's always a girl. And then he will betray her."

"Wow," she says. "That's some heavy shit."

"Shhh!" I snap. "The kids will hear you and repeat it."

"No they won't," she snaps back. "They're all the way over there."

"Those little angels could hear a squirrel fart in Maine and remember it until the end of time," I say drolly.

"Well, that's true," she laughs and then sobers. "So did he claim you?"

"Yeah," I answer.

"Do you think it'll be all right?" she asks.

"I don't know."

"Maybe ... just don't get pregnant," she adds.

"He didn't use a condom." I sigh again.

"Shit."

"Heat of the moment and all that," I say as I wave it away.

"Maybe then just don't get dead," she says.

"I'm starting to believe that that might be un-avoidable," I reply. "Are we okay?"

"I don't know," she replies, and my heart feels like it's bleeding. "I'm not going to sugar coat it, you hurt me."

"I know and I'm sorry—"

"Not yet," she interrupts me. "I'm sure you had your reasons but right now it hurts. I love you, but I'm going to need a minute."

"Okay," I whisper, trying my best not to cry on the blacktop in front of four hundred five-year-olds.

The bell to end recess rings, saving me from making a fool of myself. I nod to Amanda as my class starts to form their line to go back inside for the rest of the day.

"I'll call you when I'm ready," she says.

And that's that. I wish I could say that was as bad as my day got. But it's not.

It gets so much worse.

16

Lost and found

"I love you," she said. "And I know you had your reasons, but it hurts me that you held so much of yourself from me."

"I know," I whispered.

"I'm not going anywhere," she said. "But I'm going to need some time. I'll call you when I'm ready to talk."

"Okay." If my lip quivered a bit it's because I couldn't help it. I will say, I kept it together and didn't cry through the rest of the day.

A short time after I finished filling in Amanda on my tale of woe, the bell rang, ending recess for the day. She pulled me in for a tight hug and then hit me with some truths I knew were coming.

My lip quivered as I walked my kiddos to class.

I found the strength somewhere deep inside to keep it together for the rest of the day and managed not to cry.

I don't let the tears from when Mrs. Simmons gives me a disappointed look in the car rider line when she picks up Timmy. I can't begin to guess what that is about. It's not like I've encouraged her husband's advances; I've done nothing but shut them down.

I'm usually the dependable one but, today, it feels like everyone is disappointed in me. I can't stand it and it freaking hurts.

With the last kid packed safely into their parent's car, I head back to my classroom to close it up tight. Story books are back on their shelves. The desks are wiped clean and the chairs stacked on top.

I grab my tote bag and sling it over my shoulder before heading out. As I stare at my car, I know I can't go to my apartment. I need my mom. She can give the wisdom I need, so I climb in and steer toward home..

When I walk inside, she's brewing something on the stove. Her roasted vegetable soup in one pot and something magical in another on the other side. How she can manage two complicated things at the same time, I'll never know.

I can't not burn canned soup. Poor Bogey eats more take out than any human should and he's a cat!

"He, Mom," I greet her and she looks up with the same disappointed look on her face that everyone else has had for me today.

"Oh, honey," she says.

"What now?" I ask before I can think better to guard my tongue.

She narrows her eyes on me. "Well, I was going to soften the blow but if you're in a mood then I'll just come right out and say it," she snaps.

"Say what?" I ask on a sigh.

"You fucked up. The cards say so."

"I know. I hurt Amanda and I hate it."

"You also hurt your mate and yourself."

"Not this again," I roll my eyes.

"Yes, this again," she snaps. "He is your mate. Without him, you're hurting."

"He's a killer, Mom. He's going to hurt me if I'm with him. In the dirt nap kind," I say sarcastically. "Even you said he's the devil."

"There are different ways to interpret the devil card," she says. "You would know that if you practiced."

"No, if I practiced the whole eastern seaboard would be swallowed up by a rogue tidal surge."

"So, you're not still dreaming of Hunter?" she asks.

"Oh, I'm dreaming of him murdering me every night," I snap. "That's why I can't sleep."

"I'm sorry, honey," she says after blowing out a breath to center herself. "I made you some balance tea."

She ladles up a cup from one of her pots for me.

I take it and breathe in the milk thistle, raspberry, and something else I can't name. I cough. The first sip is always terrible, but it goes down easier after that.

I rinse my cup in the sink and set it in the dishwasher. "What am I going to do?"

"You're going to have to figure it out for yourself, honey," she says as she ladels some soup into a container for me to take home.

"But, Mom—" I start.

"No buts. You fucked up and you're going to have to fix it on your own," she says. "And with that. I think you need to start practicing your magic. I should have pushed you years ago. Now it might be too late."

"I don't know what to do."

"You'll figure it out," she says, handing me the soup. "Never forget that I love you."

"I love you too."

"And remember, whatever the Goddess wills, we accept. We don't dishonor the Goddess," she admonishes before she gently closes the door in my face.

And with that, I head home.

I don't find Hunter's magic parking karma so

I have to walk a block and a half to my building. I do at the little bodega on the way and buy a loaf of crusty bread and a bottle of wine to go with my soup. Bogey is not going to be impressed with vegetable soup so I also grabbed him a can of tuna.

I avoid small talk with Mr. Hernandez, the man who owns the bodega and always visits with me when I pop in. He would be able to tell that I had heartbreak written all over me. Whether it's best friend heartbreak or man trouble heartbreak is yet to be determined. Either way, he'd still know.

I walk the rest of the way to my building barely keeping it together. I feel lost. I'm so alone. I barely know Hunter so it can't be that I'm missing him, can it? More likely I'm smarting because I can't talk to Amanda about it. She's holed up with her own hot guy and doesn't want to talk to me because I've lied to her for years. I can't really blame her either.

My heart pangs with every step as I climb the stairs to my floor. I fumble with my tote bag and my shopping bag, looking for my keys, and I end up dropping everything to the floor. I hear my phone ringing in my bag but there's no one I want to talk to, so I let it ring.

Everyone I love, I've chased away. Chances are it's someone wanting to talk to me about my extended car warranty that I didn't buy.

I find my keys in the heap on the hall floor and

scoop everything up after I unlock the door. Bogey is sitting on the back of the sofa staring at me. Judging me. It figures that even my cat would be disappointed in me tonight. Everyone else is.

"What?" I ask as I drop my tote bag on the table by the door and move into the kitchen.

"Merow."

I let out a frustrated breath as I drop my shopping bag on the kitchen counter just as my phone begins to ring again. "Really, they should know by now I can't afford a fake car warranty."

I walk back through my living room to grab my phone. I'll just turn it off and go heat up the soup my mom sent home with me. I dig through my bag and find it at the bottom.

I have several missed calls from Hunter. He's been trying to reach me all day, but I don't know what to say to him, what to do. I'm drawn to him, but I can't stop seeing him murder me in my dreams.

At night, when he holds me under, the water filling my lungs and forcing all of the air out, my drowning feels so real. I don't know what to do.

I carry my phone with me back into the kitchen. I should turn it off like I said I would, but I just can't. I want to be close to him even though I know that I shouldn't. There's a part of me that just can't seem to cut off the connection as small as it might be.

It dings in my hand as a text comes through.

DETECTIVE BUCHANNON: Please baby, you gotta talk to me.

My fingers hover over the screen.
I want to tell him yes.
I want to tell him no, to leave me alone.

The dots blink on the screen, dancing, flirting with me as he types out another message. Maybe he's giving up on me. That would put us both out of our misery. Or maybe it would make it all so much worse. I just don't know.

DETECTIVE BUCHANNON: I need to see you.

It's so tempting. I could tell him to come over and fall into bed with him. It wouldn't take much. His earthy smell, the glint in his eyes as he looks at me. I don't know. Anything really. I could let him pleasure me in ways I've never experienced before. The way that he took me before was wild, primal even. No doubt it would be like that with him always.

But I can't. Instead, I lock my phone and set it face up on the counter because I can't help myself. I have to see if he sends another message, if he calls. I have to let the blade for that particular torture sink into my flesh, feel it cut deep.

I open the container of soup and pour it into a saucepan. I light the range, stirring the fraagrant broth occasionally. I pull the tub of margarine from the fridge. I rip a hunk of bread off the baguette I bought from Mr. Hernandez and slather it with fake butter before taking a big bite.

If ever there was a night for carbs and wine, it's tonight so I pop the cork on the bottle of red I also bought and pour it into a large wine glass. I turn off the range and ladle some soup into a bowl to eat at the counter.

My phone doesn't ring again. No messages or calls. Hunter must have given up on me for the night. And why does that hurt so much?

I'm just settling in for a long, lonely night alone when there's a knock at the door.

Mom must have decided that she wasn't really going to leave me alone to figure out my life. She never could stay mad at me for long. It helps that I was a good child. We've always been close. So when I was just a little bad, she could never stay mad at me for long.

Maybe she didn't plan to leave me to my own devices at all. She did send me with a rather large container of her soup. She probably just wanted to teach me a lesson. Well, lesson learned!

I smile to myself as I pull open the door and when I do the smile slides right off my face because standing on my doorstep looking like sex and sin is none other than Detective Hunter Buchannon.

He's in jeans that are worn and comfortable and mold to his long legs in the best of ways leading down to a pair of black boots. His gray t-shirt is stretched tight across his chest and shoulders showcasing his arms as they hang down at his sides. But it's his piercing blue eyes that cut me to the quick.

"Did you lose your phone?" he asks. His voice is pitched low and rumbles with lust and anger.

"Pardon?"

"I'm assuming you lost your phone because you sure as fuck didn't answer it," he snaps.

"Uhh … no."

"Did it fall off the fire escape?"

"No."

"Or get flushed down a toilet?"

"Also, no."

"Were you accosted by highwaymen who stole it along with your life's savings?" he asks making me laugh.

"No."

"So then you wanna tell me why the fuck you're not answering it when I call you because I've been scared as fuck that something has happened to you for two goddamn days now," he says as he pushes his way into my apartment.

"I'm … uh … not sure you should be here," I whisper as I back into a corner. I don't want to turn my back on him.

This man, for as much passion and pleasure as he's given me, is a predator. I need to be on guard when he's like this. Or maybe just in general.

"You're not sure I should be here?" he asks as he prowls around my space and then he seems to take in where I am, cornered and his anger seems to ratchet up several notches.

"No," I whisper.

"You wanna tell me why you look scared as fuck of me right now?"

"Also, no."

"You have to know that I would never hurt you," he says as he approaches me.

I hold my breath until it burns in my lungs. "I don't really know you at all," I say and then wonder why in the world I would egg on a killer who wants me to think he cares for me. Clearly, I should be locked away. Maybe I deserve to have him take me out because I'm so monumentally stupid. Too stupid to live apparently.

"I'm your mate," he replies.

"So you've said."

"You feel it," he says as he takes my hand and places it over his heart. "This connection between us. I know that you feel it too. I can't stay away from you, I need you. And I know you need me too. I can smell it on you."

"Well, whether or not I need you doesn't matter."

"What's that supposed to mean?"

"I know," I say, deciding in for a penny, in for a pound. "You're a killer."

"You're rejecting me because I'm a wolf?" he asks, letting go of my hand like it burns him. "I didn't know you were so judgmental."

"That's because I'm not," I snap.

"Well you sure could have fooled me."

"It's not because you're a wolf," I reply. "It's because I know you're a murderer. I've seen it with my own eyes … well sort of."

"What the fuck are you talking about?" he barks.

"I dream about you," I tell him. "Every night."

His eyes take on a dreamy light as he thinks of all the dirty ways that I might dream of him. And he would be right. But he would also be oh-so wrong.

"And how do you dream of me?" he asks, voicing his X-rated thoughts.

"Every night, you come to me when I'm in the bathtub," I tell him.

"Yeah," he purrs. "Are you naked and wet?"

"Yes," I whisper.

"For me?" he asks.

"Yes."

"And then what do I do?"

"You murder me."

"What the fuck?"

"Every night I tell you that I love you and then you push me down, under the water until I can't breathe and everything goes black."

"Baby, you have to know," he says, swallowing down whatever he's feeling. "You have to know I would never do that."

"But I don't know," I answer. "I don't know you at all other than the fact that night after night, I die in my dreams. My dreams are more, you were right when you called me on it in the bar. I'm having visions and in them you murder me. So excuse me if I'm not ready to jump in your arms and pledge my undying love."

"Honey."

"I think you should go."

"No."

"What?" I gasp.

"I said no. I'm not fucking leaving because you're mine. Mine to fuck and mine to protect, not to kill. I won't ever do that."

"My dreams say otherwise."

"Then I'm just going to have to prove it to you." And then he pulls me into his arms lightning quick and crushes his mouth to mine.

If before I felt alone and lost, well now in Hunter's arms, I feel all kinds of found.

17
Primal

It takes me about two point five seconds to get with the program.

I grip his t-shirt in my hands and lean into his kiss. I open underneath him when he licks the seam of my lips and pushes in, tasting me, owning me. I whimper into his mouth and he grips my backside in both his strong hands and lifts me up into his arms. It feels like every nerve ending in my body is a live wire as the thick ridge of him behind his zipper presses into me.

"Not another wall," I pant, and he chuckles as he carries me through my apartment to my bedroom.

Hunter kicks the door closed with his booted foot before letting me slide down his hard body.

We pant as we stare at each other, frozen in the moment of whether or not we go forward or go back. Do we give in to the passion or walk away? I know which one is smart. I also know which one I want.

I open my mouth to say something, anything, when the air seems to crackle around us and Hunter … just … lunges.

He pulls me into his arms again, gripping my shirt in his fists and pulling it taught on my body. Inch by inch he drags it up over my head, exposing me to his hungry gaze. His blue eyes take in everything he didn't see the one and only time we were intimate.

My shirt flutters to the floor as Hunter pops the button on my jeans and dragging the zipper down. I swear I feel the click of each of the tiny metal teeth between my legs. He slides his palms inside the waistband and shoves the jeans to the ground, leaving me standing in nothing but my bra and panties.

I want to see him like he sees me. I want to feel him hot and hard in my hand. I need to feel him, to touch him. I grab the front of his jeans in my hands and pull hard so that the buttons pop free of their moorings and watch as the soft material parts, exposing dark boxer briefs that stretch taught over his erection.

Greedily, I shove the front of his jeans down so that his hard length springs free and I wrap my hand around him. I don't know who this person is.

It's not me. It feels like I'm on the sidelines watching myself do dirty, dirty things to him and I can't seem to stop myself. It's like a primal urge to touch him, to push him to take me, to fuck me, to make me his in all ways.

I stroke and I squeeze him. We both watch as my hand moves over his cock again and again. And then he covers my hand with his and squeezes my hand tighter around him. He shows me how he likes to be touched as he guides me to roughly pull his cock and fuck him with my hand.

His eyes heat and shimmer, and he lets his head fall back a bit as he watches me with heavy-lidded eyes. A groan slips from his lips and I think he's about to come. I can't wait to watch. It's a heady feeling knowing that I'm making him come undone like this, that I'm the one to make him lose control, to make him explode.

But then he surprises me.

"Enough," he growls as he stops my hand and for a brief second, I wonder if this is punishment for not being at his beck and call for the last twenty-four hours. Is he going to leave me wet and wanting? Because I am definitely wet and I am very wanting. Getting him off or close to it was as good as getting me off as well. It would only take the slightest touch for me to be screaming his name. "Get on the bed."

He doesn't have to tell me twice. I turn away

from him as he shoves his jeans to the floor and kicks off his boots, and scramble onto the bed on my hands and knees. I barely have my hands underneath me when he grabs me by the hips, staying my movements, and rips my panties down my legs.

My breath saws in and out of my lungs as he grips my hip tight enough to bruise and presses the pads of his fingers into my flesh. He plunges two thick fingers into my pussy as he holds me in place to take what he's giving me.

"Fuck baby," he growls. "I have to taste you."

And then he replaces his fingers with his mouth as he eats me. He plunges his tongue into me, spearing me over and over, driving my arousal higher and higher. And then he kisses his way up my spine until he covers me with his body.

I hold my breath until it sears in my lungs as I wait for Hunter to fill me. I wait and wait and then the crack of his palm against my ass fills the room and I yelp.

"That was for making me worry," he says before his hand lands on my other cheek, making my pussy clench around nothing, needing him to fill it. "That was for making me want you so badly and not letting me have you."

And then he fills me deep in one solid thrust.

"Yes," I pant as he holds me to him, pumping his hips against mine.

I push back on my hands, meeting him thrust

for thrust, fucking myself on his hard cock.

Hunter pulls me up to sit on my knees as he fucks me from below. He wraps his arms around me, holding me tight, his broad chest to my back so that I'm helpless to the pleasure he gives me.

"That's it, baby," he says as he palms my heavy breast and pinches the nipple, making me clench around him. "Take what I give you."

"Yes," I pant as he snakes his other hand down between my legs. He plays with my clit, alternating between strong strokes and pinching it, as I bear down on his cock. "Please."

"Yeah, baby," he growls. "Come for me. Come all over my cock. Drench me, squeeze me in your tight pussy."

"Hunter," I gasp his name as my climax rolls over me.

"That's it, baby," he repeats as he presses me forward to ride out my climax. "Soak my cock."

"Yes." He drives into me over and over and it's all I can do to hold onto the blankets in my fists and ride it out. "Fuck me. Please, fuck me." I beg over and over, my words nonsensical as the pleasure rolls over me and through me.

"Fuck, I love this pussy." He plunges into me faster and faster.

"Don't stop," I beg as another climax rolls into the last, this one so strong I know that it'll wreck me.

"Never," he promises. "You're mine."

"Yes."

"Say it," he demands as he drives deeper and harder still, his movements becoming erratic as his own climax begins to crest.

"I'm yours," I promise. At this point, I'll say anything to get him to put me out of my misery. There's no way I can survive more pleasure.

"Damn right you are," he growls as he wraps his palm gently around the base of my throat to hold me still, to own me and possess me as he plants his cock deep and breaks the skin of my shoulder with his sharp teeth.

It's everything I need, the sting of his bite, the thick swelling of his hard cock inside me as he comes. And it sends me straight to bliss, screaming as I come.

18

Meat

He pulls out slowly and rolls me to my back, settling me gently in his arms as he nuzzles the raw skin of my shoulder. His eyes are tender as he looks deep into mine and a flash of remorse mixes with raw male pride over his sexual prowess.

"I was rough with you," he says softly.

"Yes," I whisper back. "But I liked it."

"Me too," he rumbles as he trails his fingertips between us, down my belly, parting my thighs. My eyes are glued to him, watching as he dips his fingers into me, scooping up our shared release. Painting my thighs with it.

He does it again, and then again, before admitting, "I love the look of my cum spilling from you."

"What?" I gasp, realizing what he was saying. I know in my head, what he was doing, but my mind is weak from too many orgasms and all that is Hunter Buchannon.

"My cum," he says. "I love watching it spill from your sweet pussy. I want to fill you up with it over and over again.

"Let's go back to the part where you didn't use a condom," I say. "Again."

"Baby, you practically jumped on my dick," he says.

I can hear the arrogant smirk in his voice before I look at his face. "Pardon me?"

"Pen, you were just as hot for me as I was for you," he explains. "It's part of the mating pull."

"Well, stop it."

"I can't."

"Try," I demand before rolling from the bed. "No more sex without condoms. Actually, no more sex period. That thing is dangerous!"

Hunter laughs as I snatch his t-shirt up from the floor and pull it over my head. I feel sad that I missed him taking it off. I bet that was a sight to behold. *No! Bad Penelope! No more sex with the sexy wolf.*

"Stop laughing!" I shout from the bathroom.

"I can't, baby," he says with a sweet smile that would temp a nun out of her panties. "You're just too cute."

"Am not."

"You are. Come back to bed," he says. "This time I want to take it slow."

"No," I blurt out before I can think to guard my words. "I need sustenance. You interrupted my dinner."

"But it was a nice interruption."

"We'll see," I mutter. "If an interlude turns into eighteen to life."

"Come on," he says all too sweetly as he comes up behind me. "You'd be beautiful with your belly swollen with my pups."

"Ohmygod," I whisper. "You can't be serious."

"I am," he says. "Baby, you're my mate but more importantly, you're mine. One day we're going to have a baby and if the way we come together has anything to do with it that day will come sooner than later."

"No!" I snap. "No more sex. Sex is bad."

"No can do baby, because the way you light up for me when I get my cock in you is a sight to behold," he says. "I just had you and I'm already hard for you again."

"Soup!" I shout when I feel the hard ridge of his cock pressed into my back. I want him all over again. I want to melt into him and let him have me. Maybe I'll never come up for air. Maybe I don't need to.

"Okay Penelope," he says with an all-too-knowing look in his eye. "What kind of soup are we eating?"

"Roasted vegetable," I tell him as I pull another bowl down from the cupboard. Dinner is safe. Sex is not. So I'll grasp this new opportunity for safety with both hands.

I hand him a bowl and a spoon and watch him take a bite and then another. He swirls his spoon in his bowl a couple of times before asking me, "Where's the meat?

I blink a few times because I thought by the name that would be self-explanatory, but apparently it's not.

"There is none."

"Like, none at all?" he asks.

"Like, none at all," I reply.

He doesn't answer. Instead, he quietly eats his soup so I follow his lead and eat mine too, standing in the kitchen wearing nothing but his t-shirt while he's wearing nothing but halfway buttoned jeans. It's surreal. The intimacy between us is comfortable and peaceful while the passion we share crackles in the background, like a pot set to simmer. It's not at the forefront, but it's not gone either.

When my spoon hits the bottom of my bowl, he turns to me and asks, "Are you done?"

"Yeah."

He quietly takes both bowls and spoons to the sink and rinses each item before putting them in the dishwasher. His silence suddenly makes me nervous. Did he not like the soup? Does he need some kind of meat to survive? I don't know but the idea that he's unfulfilled has me wracked with nerves.

"I could make you a ham sandwich or something," I offer him.

"Later," he says, turning back to where I stand at the counter.

"It's not bother," I say. "I can do it now."

"I said later."

"Why?" I ask and watch with rapt fascination as his eyes heat again.

"Because there's something else I want to eat right now and I'm going to take my time," he replies and then he lifts me up onto the counter and strips off the shirt I had stolen from him.

He drops his mouth to my breast and draws my nipple deep into his mouth. The sensation has my hips rocking against the cool counter. He lets the tip go with a plop and leans further into me, pressing my legs open for his invasion. He draws my legs up over his shoulders and licks my seam.

I settle back on my arms and watch as he eats me. I hold on for as long as I can. He settles his tongue over my clit and pumps two fingers into me as he licks me in quick flicks. I gasp as the sensation rolls over me, driving me hard and fast toward another orgasm and I twist my fingers into his dark hair and hold him to me.

"Hunter," I gasp as he continues to torture me. "Oh God. Yes."

And then as my legs begin to shake, I come, and he rolls my clit into his mouth and sucks deep and hard, prolonging my sweet pain.

Then he releases me and drops my legs as he stands. He pops the last remaining buttons on his jeans and lets them sink low on his hips as he lines the flush head of his cock up to my opening and slowly sinks deep inside me.

Hunter rolls his bottom lip between his teeth and bites down as he draws back and then thrusts deep inside me, again and again, at a painfully leisurely pace.

"Hunter," I beg as I sit up and wrap my arms around him.

"Penelope," he taunts before he leans back down and takes my breast into his mouth again. He draws it deep and then releases it with a hard nip to the very tip of my nipple, making me clench and gasp.

He looks down at me with a knowing smirk on his face as he swivels his hips against me, raking the base of his cock against my sensitive clit.

I scrape my nails down his back before stopping on the firm globes of his ass and pulling his hips to mine, driving him deeper inside me.

"Yes," I gasp. This new angle has him hitting something deep inside of me.

"That's right baby," he growls as he swivels his hips again, this time driving a little deeper and a little harder. "That's what you do to me. That's how hard I am for you."

"Yes," I pant as I take his cock.

"Only you drive me crazy. Only you make me wild like this."

"Hunter," I gasp and then he places his hands on my inner thighs and pushes them so wide that the position makes my muscles stretch and sting. But I'm locked in his hold. I can do nothing but take his cock like he wants me to. He drives into me faster and harder than before.

"That's right," he says. "Only me."

"Only you," I repeat as he fucks me hard on the kitchen counter.

"Touch yourself for me," he demands. "Show me how you get off on my cock."

"Yes," I reply, and I've never wanted anything more as I trail my hand down my belly and over my clit. I let my hand wander and feel where we join together, slick and wet with wanting for each other before I put my fingers where I need them most and get myself off while he fucks me.

"That's it," he says. "Get off on my cock and your fingers. Show me like I showed you how you want it."

I move my fingers faster and faster. I whimper as I move closer and closer to my climax. The orgasm barreling down on us both. And then his fingers dig into my thighs, marking me as he drives deep just before his teeth grip my shoulder. This time, he doesn't break skin, but the pressure is there, reminding me of him, and it's everything. He plunges completely into me one last time and we both come.

Once we've both caught our breath, he stands up, lifting me with him, and keeping our bodies connected in the most primal of ways. I have to scramble to cling to him, afraid that I'll fall, but Hunter just smirks because he knows he would never drop me.

He makes his way back to my room and I think that he's taking us back to bed, but he moves to the other door in the hall and takes us into the bathroom. Still holding me in his arms, he leans down, dipping me backwards as he turns the taps and then shimmies the rest of the way out of his jeans, leaving them on the bathroom floor.

What he does not do is pull the tab in my small bathroom to make the water flow through the showerhead. When he steps into the tub and moves to sit down in the rising water, I panic. Clawing at his shoulders, I fight to try and get away from him. I have to. There's something I know on a cellular level that if I don't get out of this tub, I never will.

"No!" I scream.

"What the fuck?"

"Let me go," I wail as I continue to fight.

"No, baby. Never."

"Just let me go," I plead, in the fight for my life.

Hunter adjusts, realizing his mistake and starts the shower. He stands,pressing my back to the tile wall.

"Penelope, listen to me," he says softly but firm as he pushes my hair back from my face. "You're okay. I didn't realize. I know you said that you've dreamed of Sandra's death, but I didn't realize how real it was for you until now. I'm sorry. I'm so fucking sorry."

"Let me go," I whisper. Tears burn down my cheeks and I can't stop them.

"I can't do that, baby," he says gently.

"Please let me go." Somewhere along the way, I stopped fighting him. But I need him to understand. He has to let me go. If he keeps me, I won't survive it.

"I can't do that," he says quietly, just loud enough to be heard over the water. "I need you too much."

I don't say anything else. What is there left to say anyway? Nothing I say or do will make Hunter see reason. He's determined to see this through even if that means we eviscerate each other in the end.

I'm just as guilty. I still want him even though I shouldn't. Even though I know he's going to break my heart.

Good news on that front is a broken heart still beats.

Hunter gently washes me while whispering nonsensical things. I don't hear the words, only the tenor of his voice as he tries to soothe the hurt he unintentionally caused. Little does he know, it's the physical hurt that he has yet to inflict that I know will cause me the most pain.

He shuts the taps and dries us off before carrying me like a baby to bed and tucking us in. I find sleep claims me much later than I'd have him believe. But it did claim me eventually in the false safety of his arms.

When I wake in the morning, he's gone. And I'll be damned if his absence doesn't hurt more.

19

Gone

"**D**id you kiss the handsome policeman, Miss Jones?" Emily, one of my students asks when she raises her hand during circle time. Not this again.

I'd like to say that my kids aren't hyper focused on the man that's sort of in my life, but I can't. Who knew thirty five-year-olds could be like a dog with a bone?

And who knows if Hunter is even in my life? Whether that's for orgasms or to murder me or more, I don't know. All I know is that last night felt intimate and binding, like we hit a huge relationship turning point even though we've only known each other a few days. Then, when I woke up this morning, he was gone. No note, no text, no kiss goodbye. Just … gone.

"Uhh …" I start and feel like maybe I'm having a stroke. Thirty is too young for a stroke, right?

"Of course she kissed him, dummy," another student answers. "He's a policeman. He has a badge and a gun."

"I still think his gun was pretty cool," Timmy adds.

"We've already talked about this. Detective Buchannon is a police officer. It's his job to keep us safe. Guns are not cool," I interrupt them. "They are dangerous and even deadly if handled inappropriately. Right class?"

I'm answered with a chorus of "Yes, Miss Jones."

"But you did kiss him, right?" Emily asks and man, that kid is like a dog with a bone.

"Of course she did, dummy." I let out an exhausted sigh.

"Kids—" I start. You know that movie, *Groundhog's Day*, where Bill Murray wakes up to the same flipping day every day? That's what circle time feels like since Hunter Buchannon crashed into my life, which is wild because my life has been flipped upside down since.

"I'm not a dummy. You're a dummy."

"Kids—" I try again but am cut off by the bell for recess, Thank you God. "Line up and we'll head out to recess."

They line up number order all wiggly little bodies of excitement for their outside play time. When the recess and lunch bells ring, they're more like a giant litter of excited puppies than small children. And I love every minute of my time with them no matter how chaotic it may be.

I lead my class through the halls and out to the playground where I take my place over off to the side of the handball walls so that I can see them wherever they may scatter to. It never dawned on me that maybe I should find a new spot to stand while Amanda and I work out our differences. We've always supervised recess right here where I'm standing now. This is our spot. The one that we've always met up at while we watch our classes together. We specifically request that we get lunch and recess together. Admin calls us the twins. People out in life actually think we're sisters. It's that wild.

It's not until the doors open again that I realize my mistake. And then Amanda is there, holding the door open for her class to make sure no stragglers get left behind because believe me, some of these kids have no *maybe I shouldn't do that* receptor in their brains.

She looks around and her eyes lock on me standing in our spot. That saying "like a deer in headlights" describes exactly how I feel. Now that her eyes are locked on me, standing where I now realize I shouldn't be, I'm frozen. Just call me Elsa because I can't move.

Her gaze passes over my face again and she just looks so sad. And then she subtly shakes her head and turns to go in another direction. I get it, it's too soon. Her feelings are hurt and she has a right to those feelings, but—and this is a big butt, much like my own—I have a right to my feelings as well. And right now, I'm feeling like I finally trusted my closest non-family member friend with my deepest, darkest secret, one that could cause harm to my family if it were to get out, and she let me down. Maybe my caution was right after all.

Between Amanda's defection and Hunter's disappearance, I'm not sure who I have left. Everyone is just… gone.

The bell rings to end recess and I take my class back to the room. They are in a good mood and that means it's a chatty mood. I do my best to keep us on track but it's a pretty lost cause. They want to know about the policeman and his gun. And heaven help me, but I blush every time someone mentions Hunter's gun.

By the time three o'clock rolls around, I'm exhausted both physically and mentally. I have to work the car rider line again like normal. I hope things with Amanda are a little less tense. Usually we work the line together and have fun while we do. Yesterday's events were an anomaly.

I drop my keys in my jeans pocket and lead my class to the car rider line. When I get out there, we separate them into the lines they need to be in for getting on the bus. When I look up, I see Marcie, the principal of the school leading Amanda's class out. Amanda is nowhere to be seen.

I let out a heavy sigh and start pulling kids to put them in their parents' cars. Each kid gets in, one-by-one, with a smile on their faces but mine feels more and more brittle with each passing moment.

"Hey, Timmy," I say as a familiar SUV pulls up. "Here comes your mom."

He hops up and waves goodbye to his friends before wrapping his small arms around my thighs really quick. I pull open the real door and he ambles up, tossing his bag next to his booster seat.

"Hi, Mrs. Simmons," I greet as Timmy pulls his seat belt across his body.

"I see Amanda isn't here," she says caustically as she keeps her face turned forward, but her eyes are trained on Timmy and me in the rear view mirror. It's odd. "What did you do—fuck her boyfriend too?"

"What?" I ask, wondering what the hell she could be talking about. I haven't slept with anyone in years, well, not until Hunter. Oh my God. Is Hunter her boyfriend? But she's married! Granted, her husband is a jackass with wandering hands but still!

"Nothing," she replies. "Hurry up, Timmy. We have to get going."

"Yes, Mom," he says, pulling the door closed. They motor off, leaving me standing on the curb with my jaw hanging open.

When the last child is being transported home by their parent and the last bus has left the school, I head back to my classroom. Today, I take my time wiping down the desks and setting the chairs on top of the tables. I don't rush as I reshelve the books and make sure that all of the toys and other classroom items are where they go. Green crayons here, blue markers there. There's no one waiting for me, so it's not like I need to hurry.

Everything is where it belongs, and I can't procrastinate anymore. I mean, I could, but even I'm not that desperate. Although the idea does hold merit. I grab my tote bag and sling it over my shoulder as I make my way out of the school.

Traffic is a nightmare. I should really consider taking the subway if this is going to be my usual commute. I find parking a few blocks away and quickly walk to my building. I feel my phone buzzing in my bag but as the sun is setting, I'd like to get off the streets and get home. Now isn't the time to dilly dally. My grandma always calls this time of day the bewitching hour. She says this is when the balance is uneven, and mischief is more likely.

I pull open the door to my apartment building and Bogey is there to greet me, sitting on his haunches with a look on his face wondering where I've been all day.

"I know, buddy. I know," I tell him as I bend down to pet him. Scratching under his chin and behind his ears like he likes. "How's pizza sound?"

"Merow."

"I'll take that as a yes," I say as I stand up.

I drop my bag by the front door after fishing out my phone. I look at the screen as it lights up with another incoming text and, as I make my way into the kitchen, I see I have a bunch of them. They're all from Hunter.

Detective Buchannon: We need to talk.

Detective Buchannon: Look I don't have a lot of time. Why aren't you answering your phone?

I didn't answer my phone because I was busy working. He should know that.

Detective Buchannon: Are you really going to play more bullshit games, Penelope? I thought you were better than that.

What the fuck? Well now I'm definitely not going to call him right back. Instead I tap over to my phone book and pull up my favorite pizza place around the corner. I order a pizza with sausage, mushrooms, peppers, and extra cheese. And then I turn my phone off for the night. There's no one that wants to talk to me tonight. Everyone is gone—whether it's their choice or mine—and I just want to be alone with Bogey.

I pull the opened bottle of wine from my fridge and pour a heavy glass. I need to chill out, so I carry it into the living room and flop down on the couch while I wait for my pizza. I pick up the remote and flip through the channels while I sip my wine.

The buzzer chimes next to my door.

"Dinner time, buddy," I tell my cat while I buzz up the pizza guy.

A few minutes later, he's handing me my pie in exchange for a twenty dollar bill and heading back down the stairs two at a time with a "Thanks" tossed over his shoulder.

I don't even bother with a plate. I just drop the box on my battered coffee table that was a cast off from Mrs. Yee's basement and pluck up a slice. I toss bites of sausage to Bogey and zone out as the news flips by on the screen. I drop my slice of pizza back into the box with a thunk when I see Brody and Hunter on the news. It physically hurts to see his handsome face, brooding and angry, on the six o'clock news.

If this is having a mate who doesn't really want me, then count me out.

I snatch up the remote and turn up the volume. The news casters are giving a breaking news update. I know this because BREAKING NEWS flashes across the bottom of the screen in bold type.

"This just in," the news anchor says. "There is breaking news in the Sandra Robbins murder case."

"That is correct," the other anchor says. "We have it on good authority that an arrest has been made."

"And it was none other than Lieutenant Randall Cramer, the deceased's husband."

"Sarah Cramer was found in her home, at the bottom of her bathtub on February 20th of this year."

"Lieutenant and Mrs. Cramer were married for twenty-two years and to all witnesses, they appeared to be a happy couple. We know now that looks can be deceiving."

"That is correct," the first anchor says. "We had a reporter on the scene as Lieutenant Cramer has just been led out of his home in handcuffs by two of the NYPD's finest."

"Let's go to them now ..."

"Well, shit," I say to Bogey. "That's not the killer."

20
A new day

I pack away the pizza and put it in the fridge. It's a fifty-fifty chance it'll either fester and die there or Bogey and I will eat it for two more days.

I top off his food and water bowls and then top off my wine glass. I take it back to the couch where I sit down and flip through the channels looking for a movie. There's no more news on Sandra's husband's arrest or anything else to do with them.

When my glass is empty, I take it to the sink where I rinse it out and put it in the dishwasher. I shut off the lights and make my way into my bedroom. One look at the bed has my stomach twisting. The sheets and blankets are still strewn where we left them. I'm not an organized person, I'm not the kind to make my bed every morning and I never wanted to be … until now.

With a heavy sigh, I strip out of my clothes and pull on a tank and a pair of striped, girly boxer sleep shorts that tie with a big pink ribbon at the waist to hold them up. I head to the bathroom and wash my face and brush my teeth before heading back to bed.

I lay down and pull the blankets up to my chest. They smell like sex and Hunter and I want to both cry and maybe never wash them, which is disgusting, so I push the thought out of my mind with a quick sniff one last time.

I pick up my phone, turning it back on, and scroll through the text thread from Hunter.

Detective Buchannon: We need to talk.

Should I have answered my phone on the way home? My neighborhood isn't bad, but it's not Mayberry, either. Should I have risked it? Probably not, I sure as hell didn't want to get mugged because I wasn't paying attention. I have to be confident in the fact that, in that moment, I made the right decision. If Hunter really cared about me, he wouldn't want me to risk my safety, right?

Detective Buchannon: Look I don't have a lot of time. Why aren't you answering your phone?

I bet he didn't have a lot of time. He'd said Randall wasn't the killer, but he arrested him anyway. My heart pangs for the man who had to arrest his friend, but can I trust him? In my dreams he still murders me every night. Except last night. I didn't have any nightmares while I was in Hunter's arms. More to think about for sure.

Maybe I should have called him back right away. I shouldn't have called in a fucking pizza or played with my cat. This is his overreaction, but this is my fault too. Maybe it's a sign. Maybe it's a sign that we shouldn't be together at all. It's too hard. It shouldn't be this hard to be with the person who's supposed to be your soulmate.

> Detective Buchannon: Are you really going to play more bullshit games, Penelope? I thought you were better than that.

He said he didn't have a lot of time; I bet. I guess it doesn't matter. because that last text seemed pretty final. He's done and maybe I am too. Besides, do I really want someone who accuses me of playing games? I certainly wasn't playing games, I don't do that. But the fact that dismisses me so easily hurts.

I just need a night to decompress. I trusted my best friend with my biggest secret and now she won't talk to me. The man who swore he's my fated mate might be a killer and then has the nerve to accuse me of playing games and he wasn't very nice about it.

All of that comes with some pretty heavy feelings and I need to take a minute to feel that and then deal with it. All of it. And I can't do that if everyone is mad at me. I didn't do anything wrong.

I lock my phone and set it on my nightstand. I can't keep torturing myself about would haves and should haves. I could have done a lot of things differently but the same could be said of Hunter and Amanda. It's time to put it out of my head and get some sleep. It's getting late and tomorrow is going to be another long day.

But it will also be a new day, a new opportunity to get my life back on track. I hope that it's with them, but I know now that I can't count on anyone but myself.

I toss and turn for another hour before sleep finally claims me and when it does, it's not for long.

"What?" I ask no one. A heavy pounding woke me up and it continues. "What's that?"

"Merow," Bogey complains. His sleep was just as disturbed as mine.

"I guess we should find out what the commotion is," I tell him and he just blinks his jade eyes at me. Apparently, Bogey is not on board with my plan.

I make my way into the living room. The pounding rattles my front door as someone knocks on it. What the hell? Who could be at my door at—I look at the clock on the cable box—three in the morning? This is bananas.

I pull open the door and Hunter is there, his face filled with thunder as he glares at me.

"What—?" I start to ask him what he's doing here so early in the morning, but I don't get the rest of the question out as he puts a heavy hand to my belly and gently shoves me back into my apartment. "Now wait a minute."

"No," he growls as he shuts the door behind him and throws the lock. "You do not get to talk now. The time for you to talk was when I fucking called you—repeatedly—and you didn't answer."

"But—"

"I said no," he snaps. "I'm pissed at you."

"Hey—"

"And it's late," he says as if I hadn't said anything at all. "I'm tired and I'm pissed at you. Now, we're too new to have an angry fuck and honestly I'm too angry to be careful with you, so we'll cool our heads and I'll make love to you in the morning."

"Pardon?"

"I think I was pretty clear," he says as he corrals me toward my bedroom where he strips off his clothes and climbs into my bed, leaving me standing, staring like an idiot.

"Wh-what are you doing?"

"Going to bed," he answers. "Now come here."

"No, I think we should talk," I tell him.

"No," he says. "I'm too tired and too pissed at you so come to bed. We'll talk in the morning."

"I … uh … thought you said we had other plans in the morning?"

"Don't worry, baby," he purrs. "We'll talk after I have you."

"Maybe that's not a good idea," I tell him. I'm still standing next to my bed watching his powerful body recline.

"Come to bed."

"Really," I start. "I don't think this is a good idea. You said a lot of pretty mean things and I don't know if I'm okay with it all."

"I hurt you?" he asks thoughtfully.

"Well … yeah."

"Come to bed, Penelope."

"I don't know …"

He sits up. "Come to bed or I'll come to you and when I do, I'll forgo my thoughts on not fucking you in anger tonight. Instead, I'll fuck you until you decide to be sweet to me again."

"What?" I gasp.

"Choice is yours. You either come to bed or I'll come to you and fuck you until you're too tired to argue, which may be interesting because I'm fucking wiped. Then again, fucking you is no hardship, so what's it gonna be?"

"I think I'll come to bed," I whisper.

"Good choice."

I climb into bed on the far side and decide that if I just don't let him get his hands on me, maybe I'll survive long enough to stick to my guns about whether or not we're right for each other. I'll wake up early and get to school in plenty of time to prepare for my students. Or I'll treat myself to breakfast at the diner. Table for one sounds really good right now.

These thoughts go flying right out of my head when his strong arm snakes around my waist and he hauls me up against his body.

"Maybe I should fuck you sweet anyway."

"Maybe you should go to sleep."

"You first," he says, amusement in his voice.

"I am," I lie. "I'm very tired."

"Sure baby. Let's go to sleep."

He rolls into me, pinning me to the mattress on my side with his considerably heavier weight.

I don't try to fight, it would be futile if I did, so I just lay there and try to settle my thoughts. I need to get some rest so that tomorrow I'm at my best to fight for what I want and what I need.

I hear his breathing even out and feel his body settle more on mine. I wish that I could find peace that easily. Instead, I stare at the wall for another hour or so before sleep finally claims me.

My last thought for the night being that at least tomorrow is a new day and I can try again.

I'll always try again.

21

I like this

The alarm on my phone chimes but when I reach for it, I can't move. There's a heavy weight pressing me down into the mattress that completely covers my back where I'm splayed on my belly. I feel a thick ridge pressed against my backside and a hand that squeezes my breast.

"Fuck me," he groans as he buries his face in my hair. Hair that was bound into a bun when I went to sleep but is now down and a mess around my head and shoulders. "I like this."

"I need to get up."

"In a minute," he says as he rocks his hips against my backside.

I feel a tingle between my legs as he wakes me up with his ministrations. But I'm still not ready to give in. This relationship is too rocky. Even if the sex is great, maybe the rest just isn't enough.

"My alarm is going off—"

"Okay."

He reaches across me with the hand not on my breast and grabs my phone, silencing it before dropping it back to the nightstand. It misses and falls to the floor with a clatter, but Hunter doesn't stop for a beat to grab it and pick it up. Instead, he slips his hand between me and the bed, sliding right into my sleep shorts and panties. The tip of his finger hits my clit with a purpose as his body holds me prisoner.

I'm helpless to do anything but take the pleasure that he's so freely offering and before I know it, I'm panting through my climax.

I think that he's going to pull my shorts and panties down and finish what he started but he surprises me again. Instead, he slips his hand out from between my legs and makes sure my shorts are in place before landing a gentle swat to my ass.

"Shower?"

"Huh?"

"Shower? You know that thing where you stand under the water and soap up?" He laughs as he climbs from the bed.

I roll over and eye him warily.

"What about you?" I ask.

"As much as I'd love to lose myself in your

body this morning, we don't have time for that," he says. "That was for you. You have to get to work and we need to talk before we make love again."

I'm not sure what to make of this. I can't remember a time when a boyfriend gave me a freebie. It was always them asking for blowies with no reciprocation, because that's super romantic.

"What was that about?" I ask his muscular back as I follow him into my tiny bathroom where he pulls the curtain back and starts the shower.

"I told you I was going to make you sweet again," he says as he drops the curtain and stands back to face me. He takes a step toward me, and then another. I back up with each one until my backside hits the bathroom vanity. Hunter puts his hands on the counter on either side of my hips and fences me in. "Now let's talk about why you were ignoring me yesterday after what we shared the night before?"

"Um ... I wasn't?"

"You were," he says gently. "And I want to know why."

"I wasn't," I tell him and when he looks at me dubiously, I repeat it again. "Really, I wasn't. I was busy. I had to work the car rider line by myself because Amanda is pissed at me and doesn't want to talk to me. And then I found parking a million miles from my apartment but my phone rang in my bag and the sun was going down and it's not a bad neighborhood but still, why risk it. So I hoofed it back to my building and by the time I was safe inside you'd blown up my phone with angry texts so I figured what was done was done because really, if that's how you react then I don't want to be around it."

His eyes narrow on my declaration and I brace for his reaction. If the past few weeks have told me anything, it's that Hunter is very reactionary. Anything can set him off and I know for certain that I don't want to be in the blast zone.

"Really?"

"Yes." I nod.

He's not yelling or pissed and I'm not sure what to make of it. I tip my head to the side and watch him as he watches me.

"I'm sorry," he says. *Wait, what now?* "I shouldn't have sent those messages to you. I was having a bad night and when you didn't answer, I got pissed."

"I get that," I tell him. "But you being pissed doesn't give you the right to treat me that way."

"You're right," he says.

"So, then we're at an impasse?"

"No," he replies. When I don't say anything, he expounds further. "I have a temper, baby. When it blows, it blows. Just hang on."

"Just hang on?"

"Yeah."

"Until it blows?" I ask.

"That's what I said, babe," he replies, and I feel like my head is about to explode.

"That's … That's …" I pant trying to gather my thoughts before I start screaming.

"That's what?" he asks.

"Bullshit," I snap.

He throws his head back and laughs.

"I was wondering how long you'd hold that in," he says. "Turns out, not long. And baby, you gotta know I like the way you look all the time, but when you're pissed, you're a sight to behold."

"Well get ready to be amazed," I snap. "Because that is the most caveman, chauvinistic, bullshit I have ever heard in my entire—"

I don't get the rest of my tirade out because he pulls me into his arms and kisses me stupid. He licks into my mouth, tasting me, and then quickly ends the kiss before it can spiral out of control.

"I bet the shower's warm now," he says as he pulls my stolen shirt up over my head and tosses it to the floor. "Now get in."

He gently shoves me in the direction of the tub and swats my ass as I go, making me yelp.

"Hey!" I squeal.

Hunter just smirks as he drops his boxer briefs and follows me into the shower.

22

Normal

"I have to go but I'll see you tonight."

"Okay," I reply as I stand in my bra and panties with a roller brush in one hand and my hair dryer in the other. It makes my movements awkward as Hunter pulls me into his arms and, with a smile on his face, he kisses me stupid. It's amazing what a few morning orgasms can do for one's disposition.

"This is going to be good," he says against my lips.

"What is?" I ask even though I think I already know what he's going to say.

"Us. Normal," Hunter answers and I wonder if he'd really want that once he got it.

Normal is boring. Not to me, I love boring, I

live boring, but Hunter seems like the kind of guy who lives pretty fast and loose.

"What's normal?"

"Just regular everyday life," he says. "A cop and a teacher."

"Who just so happen to be a wolf and a witch?"

"Yeah, that." He laughs.

"I wonder what that feels like."

"Well, get ready to have your socks knocked off with normal," he says as he lets me go and makes his way to the bedroom door.

"We'll see …"

"We will." He winks. "And I'll talk to Brody about Amanda."

"What?" I ask, snapping back to reality. I had gotten swept away with the romance of the morning and, let's be honest, the orgasms. "No. Don't do that."

"Consider it done," he calls over his shoulder and leaves.

I can hear him moving through the apartment.

"I said no, Hunter!" I shout. "NO!"

And then the door clicks closed behind him and I go back to drying my hair with a heavy sigh. It looks like normal isn't going to be so boring after all.

After Hunter chased me into the shower, I let him soap me up, I was on a time crunch after all, and then I got swept away in the steam and the flirting and decided to return the favor for my early morning freebie. Hunter then returned the favor for my returning the favor and by the time we were done, he barely had time to grab a cup of coffee and pull on his jeans before he was leaving with plans to see me tonight.

It's not until I'm winding up the cord to my hair dryer that I realize, we never talked about the elephant in the room. Did he do it?

I think about the way that he was with me last night and this morning and how vastly it differs from the murderer of my dreams. I pull on a soft tank summer dress and my denim jacket. I slide my feet into a pair of sneakers and grab my bag on the way out the door.

I walk to my car and drive through a place to get a cup of coffee on my way to the school. I park in my usual spot and walk through the lot but as I approach the front of the school, I feel the hair on the back of my neck zing with awareness. I look back over my shoulder and see nothing.

How weird.

I put all thoughts of normal and werewolves and magic out of my head for the rest of the morning. I definitely don't think about weird feelings and being followed as I teach my class.

When the recess bell rings, I lead the kids out to the blacktop and find another spot to stand. I give Amanda the space she asked for but it diesn't matter.

She's nowhere to be found.

23

Later

"**H**ey Penelope," Mr. Simmons says as he pulls up to pick up his son.

"Hi Mr. Simmons."

"We talked about this, Penelope."

"We did," I reply noncommittally as I turn to his son. "Have a good weekend, Timmy."

He climbs up and I close the door behind him as he buckles his seat belt.

I'm almost home free but then his dad rolls down the passenger window.

"Any plans this weekend?" he asks.

"Yes."

"A date?" he pushes, and I feel myself bristle. It's none of his business. He consistently makes me uncomfortable and I don't know what to do about it.

"Yes," I say through gritted teeth.

Something about his entire demeanor changes. He's mad and I don't understand why, but I'm mad too. He's made this obsession with me a problem with his wife, my student's mother, and honestly, I'm angry about it. This is not going to happen. He needs to let it go.

"Well, I'll see you around," he says.

I nod my head once and then he speeds away and I finally breathe a sigh of relief. Timmy was the last kid to be picked up, so I head back to my classroom to grab my belongings and pick up a bit.

Amanda was out all day today and I'm worried about her. Is she sick? Did her werewolf eat her? I don't know, and she's mad at me so I can't call her up and ask.

Or can I?

I sling my tote bag over my shoulder and head out to the parking lot. I climb in my car and start home. I have no idea what Hunter's plans are other than he said he'd see me tonight. Does that mean a date? Dinner? He's coming over for sex after all of those things? I just don't know.

The only thing that does go right today is my finding a parking space on the street only two blocks away from my building. I grab my keys and my bag and take the brisk walk home after locking up my car.

I jog up the stairs to my apartment and let myself in. Bogey is nowhere to be found. I grab my phone and set my bag down by the door before kicking off my shoes. I dial Amanda's number and make my way into the kitchen. Her phone rings and rings and rings until, finally, her voicemail picks up.

"You've reached Amanda. I can't get to the phone right now so please leave a message and I'll get back to you as soon as I can. Bye!"

"Uh, hey Amanda. It's me," I stammer. "You weren't at the school today and I was worried. So I just thought I'd call and check in. Call me back when you get a chance ... or ... uh ... don't? Gotta go. Bye."

"Or don't?" I say out loud to no one. "What an idiot. No wonder I have no friends."

I set my phone down on the counter and pull open the fridge for my bottle of wine. I pop the cork and pour myself a glass, but it holds no interest. I'm just feeling sorry for myself tonight. In the end I pour it down the drain and set my glass in the sink.

I settle onto the couch and grab the remote. Flipping through the channels, I find nothing that holds my interest until I settle on a RHONY marathon. There's just something about the Real Housewives of New York that make me feel better about my life.

Bogey wanders out and curls up at my side. I silently stroke his plush coat as we watch a bunch of wealthy middle-aged women behave badly. I can't think of a better way to spend my evening. If I get hungry, I'll order Chinese. But until then, I'm all right just like this.

Sometime after the housewife with short hair goes to rehab, there's a knock on my door. Shit. I had forgotten all about my date with Hunter.

Bogey settles back into the sofa after I jump up and head toward the door. I pause in front of it and brush my hair back from my face before reaching for the handle.

When I pull the door open, Hunter is standing there looking gorgeous in a pair of tailored gray slacks belted at his trim waist, a blue shirt that sets off his eyes is open at the collar, and a dark blue sport coat.

I have to blink to get my thoughts back in line, which is why I miss him move. He surprises me when he lunges and pulls me into his arms, kissing me stupid. I'm helpless to do anything other than open my mouth under his and whimper when he licks in, touching his tongue to mine.

When Hunter finally ends the kiss and pulls back, I lose my balance as the room swirls around me. He has to grab me by my arms to steady me.

"Hey." I breath like an idiot, making him smile a blinding smile at me.

"Babe," he laughs.

"What?"

"I thought we talked about you answering your phone when I called."

"We did," I answer and then it dawns on me what he's saying. "You didn't call."

"I did."

"Shit," I whisper. "I left it in the other room. I must not have turned the ringer back on after work. I'm sorry."

"It's okay," he says.

"I really am sorry."

"I know honey," he replies gently. "Ready to go to dinner or did you already eat? I left you a message but I'm getting that you didn't get it."

"I didn't," I answer. "And I also didn't eat."

"Then let's go," he says, leading me back to the door.

"Um …" I start.

"What's bothering you?"

"Well …" I hedge. "You're dressed really nicely and I'm kind of not." I point out his nice clothes and my dress. He looks like he's ready for someplace fancy and I am lucky there are no handprints in washable paint all over me. It's happened before.

"Baby, you look beautiful," he says. "I just want to be with you. Wherever that might be. So let me take you to dinner?"

"Okay."

"Good," he says before placing a quick, hard kiss on my lips.

Hunter pulls open my front door and holds it for me as I slide my feet back into my chucks and pull on my cute jacket. I grab my bag and let Hunter lead me to his SUV. He pulls open the passenger door for me and I climb up before he shuts the door behind me. I watch the powerful moves of his body as he strides around the hood of the vehicle and climbs in.

"What do you feel like?" he asks me.

"Anything, really."

"Chinese?" he suggests, and I burst out laughing. "What?"

"That's what I was thinking of calling in tonight if you were going to be late," I admit.

"Great minds. I know just the place."

I don't say anything as he drives to a swanky place across town. I'm not ready to take him to Mrs. Yee. Besides, that would be like having a first date with my grandma, for all intents and purposes.

This is just for us.

We'll bring the families in later if everything works out.

I know he said we're a sure thing, but I'm not so convinced. Until then, I'm happy to play things by ear. I'm still smarting from the sting of his brutal words from last night. His sweetness this morning made up for some of it, but I'm not the kind of woman to give verbal abuse a free pass for candied words the next day. I need actions, not empty promises.

He pulls into a parking lot in front of a modern designed building and parks the car.

"Wait here," he says as he pulls his keys from the ignition and walks around the hood of the car. He pulls open my door for me and offers me a hand to help me down. The loose skirt of my dress rides up around my thighs and my breath catches in my throat as I watch his eyes flash with lust and heat as they trail back up my body to my face. "Later."

"Thanks," I whisper as I slide down from the SUV and he closes the door behind me.

"Anytime," he says, his voice rumbling with the double meaning behind his words.

I feel my nipples pebble in my bra but I roll my shoulders back and steel my spine instead. Sex isn't the problem with us, it's everything else. If we fall into bed every five seconds, we won't have a relationship at all. Then again, if the Jones curse holds strong, we won't have one anyway.

Hunter takes my hand in his and leads me to the huge glass doors at the front of the building. He pulls one open and holds it for me. The hostess smiles brilliantly at my handsome date and then she seems to dim a bit when she notices me.

"We have a reservation for two," he says smoothly. "Buchannon."

"Yes, Mr. Buchannon," she says as she scoops up some menus. "Right this way."

She leads us to a dimly lit booth in the back of the restaurant. Hunter and I follow her with his hand burning a place on the small of my back. Everything about my body reaches for him and it's completely juxtaposed to the way that my brain tells me to run for my life. I just don't know what to do about it.

"Penelope," a voice I didn't expect to hear calls my name as we pass a table. I look over to see Mr. Simmons and a young blonde sitting across from each other at an intimate table. "What a surprise."

"Yes," I respond, and Hunter stiffens beside me. It's almost as if I can see each muscle in his body pump up one at a time. "Have a good evening."

"You too," he says as we walk away.

I sit down on one side expecting Hunter to slide in across from me. He does not.

He pushes me through to the wall, his body crowding me in on one side. He takes both menus from the young hostess and hands me mine.

"Thank you," I say to her to try and smooth things over because he's made it awkward.

"Your server will be with you shortly."

"What's good here?" I ask him quietly.

"You've never been here before?"

"No."

"The mu shu chicken is fantastic," he says. "I like the lemon chicken with peas and rice, as well."

"That sounds good."

"How do you know that man?" he asks casually. In fact, it's so casual that I'm not even sure it's a thing. But I know better. I chance a quick look at him but his face is blank. Hunter's face is never blank. This question is more important than he wants me to believe.

"He's the father of a student," I reply just as casually.

We're not in a place where we trust one another, that much is clear. So I can't tell him that Mr. Simmons has been making me feel uncomfortable for the better part of a year. That it's been bordering on sexual harassment lately and has become a strain between me and his pregnant wife.

"That's all?" he asks as a waiter comes to the table to take our drink order.

"What can I get you to drink tonight?" he asks as he set down little pots of dipping sauce and a bowl of fried wonton strips.

"A bottle of white wine," Hunter asks.

"Very good. I'll be back in just a moment."

"Yes, that's all," I answer when the waiter is away from the table.

"Hmm," he says, taking my hand in his. He plays with my fingers as I look over the menu.

"Here we are," the waiter says as he brings a

bottle to the table and two glasses. He pops the cork and fills a glass. Hunter takes it from him and hands it to me. I have to set my menu aside to take it from him because he won't let go of my other hand.

"Thank you."

"Have you had enough time to decide," the waiter asks.

"Have you had enough time to decide?" Hunter asks me as he looks me in the eyes.

I feel like there's more behind his words than just what I'd like to eat but I don't know what to do about that, so I order instead.

"Yes."

"What would you like, love?" Hunter asks me softly as he raises our linked hands to brush the backs of his knuckles against my cheek. The move is very intimate and makes my face heat.

"The lemon chicken please."

"I'd like the mu shu chicken, hot and sour soup for both, fried rice for her, steamed for me, wont-ons, and spring rolls, please," Hunter orders as he passes our menus to the waiter.

"Coming right up."

"That's a lot of food," I say, grasping at any-thing to break the mounting sexual tension be-tween us.

He smiles broadly, obviously knowing what I'm up to.

"We eat a lot," he replies. "Whatever you don't eat won't go to waste. But I want to take care of you. I *need* to take care of you."

"There's a lot to unpack there," I say and he's just about to reply when a shadow appears at our table.

"Having a pleasant evening, Penelope?" Mr. Simmons asks. The way that he says my name is overtly sexual and makes me uncomfortable.

Hunter looks ready to leap across the table. I place my hand on his thigh to steady him and he seems to calm down, barely.

"Yes, thank you."

"I didn't expect to see you here tonight," he says, and I wonder if he's afraid that I'll tell his wife.

"No." Maybe if I keep things as vague and bland as possible, he'll go away and my date won't try to kill him later.

"You look lovely tonight," he says. "You were lovely in that dress earlier and I'm sure you'll be even lovelier later out of it."

"Excuse me," I gasp.

"I'll be seeing you, lovely Penelope," he purrs and with that he walks back to his table with a smug smile on his face.

"You want to tell me what that was about?" Hunter quietly snarls.

"No."

"Wrong answer," he warns.

"I can't because I have no idea what that was," I say, letting out a heavy breath. "Let's just try to have a nice dinner. Okay?"

"All right, mate," he says. "But fair warning, I'll not share."

"I'm not yours to own, Hunter."

"That is where you are very wrong, my sweet mate."

"Here is your soup and spring rolls," the waiter says, breaking the tension between Hunter and myself as he sets the plates and bowls down on the table. "Your dinner will be right out."

I spoon up sips of soup and close my eyes as the bursts of flavor pop on my tongue. When I open my eyes, Hunter is watching me with a look of hunger on his face. He quickly wraps his hand around the back of my head and leans in swiping his tongue across the seam of my lips as he kisses me.

"Mm," he says. "It is good."

He's so over the top ridiculous I can't help but laugh. "You know you have your own soup," I tell him.

"I do but it tastes better mixed with you."

I feel those words between my thighs and squirm a bit in my seat. This time it's Hunter's turn to laugh at my discomfort. He offers me a bite of spring roll from his fingertips and I take it, making sure to swipe the pad of his digit with the tip of my tongue. Two can play this fun game.

The waiter quietly brings our meals and leaves again. Hunter and I take turn sharing bites of food with each other along with quick kisses and slightly less than innocent touches.

I drink more than my fair share of the wine as Hunter is driving. He only indulges in one glass, but the bottle is empty by the time that he pays our bill.

I feel warm and fuzzy from the wine but not drunk. Relaxed and content from the easy banter and play with Hunter as he leads me through the restaurant and out to his SUV.

He opens the passenger door for me and lifts me up by the waist to place me on the seat, making me giggle. Okay, maybe I am a little drunk, but I don't care. It's been a great date so far.

He leans into me, standing in the door of the car and brushes his nose down the side of my face while he lays his palm heavy on my thigh. "See? I told you it would be good," he whispers in my ear.

"What's that?" I ask. My voice is breathy from the wine and the sexual tension we've been building up between us all night.

"When your mate takes care of you," he says, his voice rough. "Now your mate is going to take you home and take care of you in other ways."

"Okay," I breathe and then gasp as he nips my ear before stepping back and shutting my door.

Hunter walks around the hood of the car and climbs in the driver's seat. He starts the car and then grabs my hand, pulling it across the space between us to play with my fingers as he drives back across town.

In a way that only happens for Hunter, someone pulls out of a curbside space as he pulls up to my building and he parks right by the door. I let us in and together we walk up the stairs to my door. I pull the keys from my bag and he takes them from my hands and lets us in. He closes the door behind us and turns the heavy lock with a loud snick.

"Now baby," he rumbles.

"What?"

"It's later and I'm hungry."

"How can you still be hungry?" I ask as I drop my bag on the table by the front door.

"I'm not hungry for food," he growls. "I'm hungry for you."

"Oh," I whisper.

"Yeah, 'oh,'" he growls. "Now lift up that skirt that's been teasing me all night and show your mate your pretty pussy."

His dirty words mix with the sweet wine and now I want nothing more than to do exactly what he's told me to. I push my jacket down my arms and toss it aside as I kick off my sneakers. And then I slowly gather the seafoam green jersey material in my hands until the hem rises up over my belly button so that he can see how soaked the gusset of my cotton panties is.

"Yes," he groans as he drops to his knees in front of me in the middle of my living room and buries his nose between my thighs, breathing deep. "Fuck. I love the way you smell. Tell me it's just for me, mate."

"It's just for you," I whisper the truth. During sex I can be laid bare for him in ways I'm not prepared to be with clothes on.

"I have to eat you," he growls as he pushes my panties down my legs.

"Yes."

He nudges my feet wider and rests his large hands on my thighs, parting me with his thumbs leaving nothing to protect me from the harsh swipe of his tongue on my clit. My knees buckle and my legs threaten to give out but he holds me up to take his sensual assault.

I shove my fingers through his hair and pull. I don't know whether I'm trying to push him away or pull him closer as he gives me no quarter. He licks and nips and sucks me, as he fucks me with his tongue.

And when I can take no more, I come with a gasp. My breath is sawing in and out of my lungs and my pussy still spasms around nothing as Hunter stands so fast the room spins. He scoops me up and I wrap my legs around his waist, clutching his shoulders as he stalks toward my bedroom.

He lays me down in the middle of my bed and straddles me as he pulls my dress up over my head, leaving me laying there in nothing but a pale lace bra. He jerks each button on his shirt free from its mooring and I can't help but run my hand over the large bulge in the front of his slacks.

With a rumble from deep in his chest he tosses his shirt to the floor and then quickly unbuckles his belt and unzips his pants, letting the material part to show the thick ridge of his erection as it tests the bounds of his underwear.

Fast as lightning, he flips me to my belly and pulls my knees up underneath me. He keeps my breasts and cheek pressed flat to the bed leaving the very heart of me exposed to him. I barely catch my breath when he surges over me and plunges deep inside.

He gives me no chance to adjust to his size as he thrusts deep and hard, holding me open to his onslaught. I'm helpless to do nothing but take it and I revel in it. I feel so full of him as he takes me with deep strong strokes and before I can stop it, I'm hurtling toward another climax.

Fortunately, I have nothing to worry about because Hunter is with me to the end.

I feel his cock swell inside me as he strikes, biting my shoulder, marking me as his again. It's everything I need to send me over the edge and I come on a scream. He drives deep one last time and fills me up as he comes.

His arms tighten around me in an embrace. "I didn't mean to be so rough with you again," he says.

"Maybe I like it when you're rough." It's easier to say the honest things when I'm not looking at his deep blue eyes and all of the emotions that swirl behind them.

"I also meant to take my pants off," he says as he pulls out of me and rolls me over.

"There's always next time," I say breezily as I watch him kick off his pants and palm his still hard cock that glistens with our cum.

"There's always now," he says as he covers me with his hard body and slides deep.

"What about now?" I gasp as he glides out and pushes deep inside again as if he has all the time in the world.

"Now's the time for me to make love to you."

"Okay," I whisper as he draws out each move, sliding through my swollen and sensitive folds.

"Now kiss me, love."

"Okay," I breathe as I use my abs to lean up and press my mouth to his.

Hunter wraps his arms around me as he rocks our bodies together in a rhythm as old as time. Gently, softly, we kiss and touch each other as we come together. While before was hard and fast, this time he draws out each bit of pleasure, making it last until well into the night.

And then finally, with our arms wrapped around each other, I gasp against his lips as I come. Hunter plants himself deep inside me one last time and whispers my name to the night as he finds his own release.

Not much later, he slides from me one last time, and turns me so that I'm cocooned in his arms as he spoons me. He draws the covers up over our bodies and I drift off into a peaceful sleep in the safety of his arms.

Too bad it's not meant to last because it was a great night, and if I let myself, I could get used to this.

24

Dreams

Naked. I am naked and in a large bathtub. The steam from the water rises up and fills the room as the tub slowly fills around me. The sound of the water running relaxes me after a difficult night at home. The anger that fills me when I think about my husband and how he doesn't appreciate me anymore. All I ever wanted was for Randall to love me. To want me. But I guess I was asking too much.

The door clicks as the knob turns from the outside and the door is pushed open. I wonder if maybe I finally got through to Randall and he decided to surprise me now, in the middle of the day.

But when the door opens completely, it doesn't reveal Randall, but someone else entirely. Someone *who knows me more intimately than Randall. I'm sad that my husband doesn't want me like he used to but this one does and I've decided to grab hold of the opportunity. Maybe this is my second chance at happiness.*

"Hey," he says with a smile on his face.

"Hi," I reply. "I didn't expect to see you to-day."

"I just couldn't stay away," he says as he pulls his polo shirt up over his head and drops it to the counter.

"Is that so?" I ask as I snuggle down into the warm water, hoping he likes what he sees as much as I know he does.

"Absolutely." he drops to his knees next to the tub and reaches into the water with a strong hand, dropping it instantly between my spread thighs.

He toys with me, his fingers moving over me before thrusting two deep inside, making me gasp.

"Mm," I purr as he takes me higher. Then, without warning, he withdraws his fingers from my core and I snap my eyes open. "What are you do-ing?"

"I'm sorry, Sarah," he says as he pushes up to stand over me.

I move to cover my nudity with my hands but what I should have done was ward off an attack. Feeling humiliated that now not one, but two men in my life want nothing to do with me, I just want to curl up and hide.

I never see him coming.

Before I know it, his hand wraps around my neck and squeezes. I gasp for air and I'm sure confusion glitters in my eyes. He doesn't seem confused at all as he pushes me under the water.

I pull and scratch at his hands and arms but it's no use. He won't let me go.

My lungs burn. I can't hold my breath any longer.

Bubbles pop out of my mouth as the air rushes out and the water rushes in. And then I let go and everything just ... fades away into nothingness.

I gasp as I try to fill my lungs. They burn. The oxygen sears through them as I try to draw more and more into my body but it's no use. I'm drowning.

"Penelope, baby, what the fuck?" Hunter barks into the night and my eyes pop open.

I'm still gasping for breath. I'm drowning.

"Baby, what's happening?" he asks and I shove away from him and scramble backward up the bed on my hands and feet like a crab to get away from him. "Penelope?"

"No," I bark. My voice sounds harsh to my own ears and Hunter's eyes go wide when he hears me. "Stay back."

"Baby, come here."

"No." I'm cornered. I need to get away.

All the time he was showing me what a sweet guy he was, he really wasn't. Hunter was always a murderer. The Devil. The card my mom turned over and over. He was always meant to kill me. I knew it. She was so sure the curse would be broken with me, that Hunter was a knight in shining armor but he was always sent to kill me.

"Baby. I said come here," he growls out his command.

Grandma said we should trust the fates, but they were playing me cruelly all along.

"Please," I beg. "Let me go."

Something hard changes across his face. He's angry. The game is over too soon and now it's time for me to die.

I know it.

He knows it.

Now the only chance I have left is to fight or to just let go. Can I do it? Can I just lay back and let him take my life like he took Sandra's?

All I know is that it all ends here and now.

I can't. As he watches me in the dark with his preternatural vision, I know that I can't do it. I can't sit back and let him snuff out my light without a fight, even though I know it will be futile.

He's stronger than me and he's faster than me and I stand not one single chance against him because he's super natural and I'm nothing but a failure as a witch.

I roll to the side to leap off the bed. Maybe if I can get a head start, I can get out of here and find someplace safe to hide out. Maybe I can get to my mom's house. Surely, she and Mrs. Yee can protect me from my wolf killer.

I reach the end of the bed when a strong hand manacles my ankle and pulls, dragging me back across the bed.

"No!" I scream.

He flips me over so I'm flat on my back. My hair is wild around me, some falling over my face, but I can't do anything about it. Hunter has me pinned to the mattress with his heavy weight. His hands hold my wrists above my head and his feet press my ankles down to the bed. I'm not going anywhere until he lets me.

I lost.

I tried to get away. I knew that it was no use, but still. I never even had a chance.

Hot tears stream down my face. I'm not prepared to die.

He lowers his head, putting his face in mine. He's angry. It's palpable, a living, breathing thing that fills the room around us.

"Baby, what the fuck?" he roars.

"Just do it."

"What?"

"Just do it," I push. "Get it over with."

"What the fuck are you talking about?" he

roars.

"K-k-kill me."

"What?" he whispers, and this volume is even scarier than before.

I think I liked him shouting more. That was predictable, this is deadly.

"Kill me," I answer. "I know you're going to do it. I saw it again tonight. So just get it over with. Stop toying with me."

"Baby, no," he whispers. It's tortured and painful. But I can't believe his lies anymore. Hope is a bitch a of a thing. If he gives me anything to hope about, then it'll hurt worse when he turns on me later.

"Please," I whimper.

This can't go on. I can't bear the waiting any longer. I close my eyes as one more tear slips free and then I'm rolling, flying, no longer pinned tight to the bed by his anger.

Instead, Hunter holds me lovingly in his arms. He tucks my chin to the crook of his neck and rocks me gently as he strokes my hair and my back.

"Shh, baby," he whispers. "You're safe here. You're safe with me. I'll never hurt you. Never. You're my mate. Mine to protect. Shh."

But I can't stop crying. I can't catch my breath. No one will protect me. My fate is sealed. I'm meant to die by his hands. I'm not safe. I'll never be safe.

"Not safe," I try to force out but it's a struggle. I can't catch my breath and my chest tightens painfully.

"You are safe," he says. "Get some rest. I'll protect you."

"Never safe," I choke out one last time and then thankfully the darkness takes me and it's peaceful.

I gasp and twist the bed sheets in my hands as he spears me with his tongue. My legs draw up around his head on their own and he places his heavy hands on my thighs, prying them back open.

It's too much. And yet it's not enough in a way that I won't ever be complete again without him driving deep inside me, joining us as one.

"Please," I beg. For him to stop or for him to eat me alive, I don't know, only he does.

He slips his tongue from my opening and I feel empty and wanting but he doesn't make me wait long. He parts me with his thumbs and opens his mouth over me, sucking the life from me while he flicks the tip of his tongue over my clit. I let go of the sheets and drive my hands into his hair, holding him to me, desperate for more of what only he can give me.

He pulls me deeper as only he can. It's like he pulls me under the waves, and I lose my breath completely as the air rushes out of my lungs.

I shatter into a million beautiful pieces.

My heart races but I open my eyes and watch

as he kneels between my thighs and places the tip of the condom wrapper in his mouth, tearing it open with his teeth. I hear the foil crinkle as he tosses it away, where I don't know because my eyes are riveted to the veins and tendons in his tanned forearms as he rolls the latex down his impressive cock.

My mouth waters. I want it. I want him. But I won't have to wait long because he grips my thigh in his hand wrapping my leg high on his waist, while he braces himself on the other arm as he presses the blunt head of his cock to my opening and drives deep.

My eyes pop open when I feel the broad head of his cock breach my opening. He fills me quickly, not giving me a chance to adjust to the size of him. This isn't a dream. Or my dream is happening in real life. Either way, I don't know whether to be terrified or to hold on.

"Yes," I pant.

I hold on tight, his thrusts hard and fast as he sets a punishing rhythm that we both desperately need. He presses the pads of his fingers into my hips in a way that I know I'll wear his marks tomorrow. But it's the way he savagely plunges into me that lets me know I'll feel him there for days.

I feel another orgasm—this time a real one and not one in my dreams—build within me and blaze through me like an out of control rocket. But it's not enough. I need more.

"That's it, baby," he purrs as he feels me clench around him, reaching, grasping for the climax that won't come.

"Please," I beg again. "I need …"

"I know what you need," he rumbles as he lets go of my thigh and slides his hand between us so that he can finger my clit as he plunges in and out of me.

It's exactly what I need.

"Yes, yes, yes," I moan as a shudder rips through me. "I need you."

His thrusts become erratic as he drives me forward in my climax. The bed banging loudly against the wall as he does.

And then, I just let go.

He drives deep over and over and like a chain reaction, he plants himself inside me as my orgasm rips his from him.

He slowly glides in and out of my body as we come down.

"Penelope," he whispers my name.

When I open my eyes, I feel a chill in the room. Does he feel it too? The otherworldly way we came together, wild and raw? Does he know that this has happened exactly like this, only in my subconscious? Was he there? I don't know and I'm afraid to ask.

"What was that?" I whisper into the dark. I don't know what time it is, only that it's very late. Maybe in the middle of the night or not quite morning.

"I needed you," he says, his words almost identical to those of my dreams. Maybe this is how it's supposed to be, maybe the visions are changing. I'm not sure. "I always will. And I think you need me too."

I do but I'm not willing to admit it. At least, not yet.

"Let me in, baby," he whispers. Our bodies are still connected in the most intimate of ways.

I shake my head because I can't. If I let him in that means I trust him, not only with my heart but my safety and my life.

"Take down the walls, let me in."

I nod once because I just can't fight it anymore. Last night, when he defeated me so quickly, I had no choice but to give in and when I did, something in me broke. There's no getting it back now. So I'll let him in. I have nothing left to lose.

"Okay," I whisper.

"I promise that you'll never regret it," he says before pressing his mouth to mine and kissing me passionately.

"Okay."

He rolls us to our sides. I'm still in his arms and he's still inside of me. The way that he arranges us is intimate as we're intertwined but it's also comfortable.

"Sleep," he commands me gently and I'm so emotionally and physically exhausted, I do. Right there in his arms, just like he wanted.

Naked. I am naked and in a large bathtub. The steam from the water rises up and fills the room as the tub slowly fills around me. The sound of the water running relaxes me after a difficult night at home. The anger that fills me when I think about my husband and how he doesn't appreciate me anymore. All I ever wanted was for Randall to love me. To want me. But I guess I was asking too much.

The door clicks as the knob turns from the outside and the door is pushed open. I wonder if maybe I finally got through to Randall and he decided to surprise me now, in the middle of the day.

But when the door opens completely, it doesn't reveal Randall, but someone else entirely, someone who knows me more intimately than Randall. I'm sad that my husband doesn't want me like he used to but this one does and I've decided to grab hold of the opportunity. Maybe this is my second chance at happiness.

"Hey," he says with a smile on his face.

"Hi," I reply. "I didn't expect to see you today."

"I just couldn't stay away," he says as he pulls his polo shirt up over his head and drops it to the

counter.

"Is that so?" I ask as I snuggle down into the warm water, hoping he likes what he sees as much as I know he does.

"Absolutely." he drops to his knees next to the tub and reaches into the water with a strong hand, dropping it instantly between my spread thighs.

He toys with me, his fingers moving over me before thrusting two deep inside, making me gasp.

"Mm," I purr as he takes me higher but then, without warning, he withdraws his fingers from my core and I snap my eyes open. "What are you doing?"

"I'm sorry, Sarah," he says as he pushes up to stand over me.

I move to cover my nudity with my hands but what I should have done was ward off an attack. Feeling humiliated that now not one, but two men in my life want nothing to do with me, I just want to curl up and hide.

I never see him coming.

Before I know it, his hand wraps around my neck and squeezes. I gasp for air and I'm sure confusion glitters in my eyes. He doesn't seem confused at all as he pushes me under the water.

I pull and scratch at his hands and arms but it's no use. He won't let me go.

My lungs burn. I can't hold my breath any longer.

Bubbles pop out of my mouth as the air rushes out and the water rushes in. And then I let go and everything just ... fades away into nothingness.

My body jerks awake and then strong arms band tight around my body squeezing the air from my lungs. Not that there was any in there before because I was drowning. Again.

"What the fuck was that?" Hunter gasps.

"What was what?" I ask. I'm so tired of all of the questions, there's no way to explain it to him.

"You drowned," he roars. "I drowned you!"

"You saw it?" I gasp.

I've never thought that anyone would share my dreams, my visions with me. And, I'd never want them to. It's horrific. And now Hunter knows why I tried to avoid him.

"Yes," he bites out, rolling us so his body covers mine, pinning me to the bed as he holds me tight in his arms. "Is it always like that?"

I don't want to lie to him, but I don't want to hurt him either, so I go with door number one and give him the truth. "Yes."

"I'm so sorry," he pleads. "Baby, I'm so sorry."

"It's okay," I say. And while I try to comfort him, I wonder exactly why it is that I'm trying to comfort him at all for murdering me in my dreams. My life has definitely taken a turn for the bizarro and I was raised by a coven of hippie witches, so that's saying something.

"It's not," he replies. "Baby, you've got to believe me. I would never hurt you. Please believe me."

"I do." And I really do. He's so upset that I can't believe he would kill me. Then again, I've been dreaming of him as if I was the dead wife of his friend—Hunter's lover. "How long were you lovers?"

"Lovers?" he asks as if he doesn't understand.

"That's not me in the dream, Hunter," I explain.

"I don't understand."

"I'm dreaming of us but it's not me as me," I explain. "It's me as Sarah Cramer, your friend's wife. But it is you as you, so I'm asking how long you were lovers."

Hunter lets go of me instantly and rolls to the side of the bed. He sits there with his legs over the side, feet flat on the floor and his elbows resting on his knees. He hangs his head in his hands. He's upset and rightfully so. He has to have just realized that his current lover now knows that he killed his last.

"It's okay," I say softly, still trying to comfort him. "No matter what's been done, I know that you won't hurt me because you said so. You promised." Although, if I'm telling the truth, I'm still iffy here at best.

I don't know where to go from here, or what to do, what to say. Should I leave? Although that's stupid, this is my apartment.

"We don't need to talk about it," I tell him. "We can go back to bed or one of us can leave…"

"One of us?" he asks. "Penelope, you fucking live here."

"Yes."

"So you're just going to leave because you think I murdered the wife of one of my best friends?" he asks.

"Are you going to let me leave?" I ask quietly after a beat. This is the most honest, most direct I've been with him the entire time we've known each other. He could tell me no and still turn on me.

"Are you shitting me right now?" he snaps.

"Uh … no," I answer. "I'm not … shitting you?"

"Because you've got to be," he says. "There's no other way."

"I don't understand."

"Well that fucking makes two of us," he roars.

"Are … are you angry with me?" I ask.

"Yes, I'm fucking angry with you!" he shouts as he jumps up to face me from across the room. "Did it ever dawn on you that maybe I didn't do it?"

"Uh … no."

"Uh … no," he mimics. "Did it occur to you that when fate threw us together, I was all in?"

"No," I whisper.

"That I've all but told you I love you every single time we've been together?"

"No."

"While I was chasing you all over town and trying to solve the murder of my best friend's wife, did it ever occur to you that I was all in?" he roars. "That I was in love with you?"

"Are you?" I ask quietly. "In love with me that is."

"I was," he snaps. "Now I'm not so sure."

"What?" I gasp as I watch him pull on his discarded clothes with jerky movements. "What are you doing?"

"I don't know," he answers. "I just know I've gotta go."

"Wait," I plead. "Maybe we should talk about this."

"Baby, the time to talk was days ago. The time to talk was when I was knocking myself out to show you that I thought you were the one. The time is not now. Not anymore."

And with that he storms out of my apartment, slamming the door as he goes. I had thought that the Jones curse would carry out once again when he murdered me, turns out he just broke my heart instead. No, not broken. Shattered irrevocably because the mate I didn't want now doesn't want me at all.

And it hurts so fucking much.

25

Abandoned

Taylor Swift's *We Are Never Getting Back Together* blares from my phone on the bedside table. Sometime late last night while crying my eyes out, I decided that it was my new anthem and set it as my alarm tone before creating my perfect broken heart anthem with tunes like *Sail* and *Bleeding Love* along with it.

I can barely get my eyes to crack open. A pretty crier, I am not and last night was no different. I can feel how swollen and crusty they are. I grab my phone from the nightstand and tap the screen to silence Taylor's angry alarm.

It feels like I had barely fallen asleep when it sounded. I want to go back to bed so bad. I would too if it wasn't for my lesson plans. Even kindergarten is hard to have a sub jump in because they still need a heavy lesson plan for the day. Though, I do have a ton of sick leave and vacation saved up because I'm never sick and I don't ever go anywhere.

Could I? No.

But maybe? I don't know.

I've never done anything like that before. I'm always the responsible one. To be honest, Amanda is the wild child who might not show up on a Monday morning if the guy she met Friday night was particularly good with his skillset.

Maybe it's my turn. Not that I'm hooked up with a guy. Not that. Never that again. But I could play hooky.

I quickly swipe the crust from my eyes and log into the school district website to request a sub for my class. As soon as that's done and the one that I love confirms, I shoot a quick email to the principal. I tell her that I'm not feeling well and that I think it's best to just lay low and rest today. When she emails me back fifteen minutes later, she doesn't come right out and say that she doesn't believe me, only that she can't actually remember a time when I've been sick enough to call into work.

Of course, if Amanda is feeling particularly petty, everyone will know that I fucked up a good thing and chased away the only decent guy to show me any attention away as soon as she hears the news.

I turn the ringer off on my phone and toss it to the nightstand. I lay down to go back to sleep. Only I can't because I'm awake now and I have to pee. So I do what I need to and then jump back in bed and pull the covers up to my ears. Maybe all my problems will go away if I just sleep.

At some point in time, Bogey climbs up and curls into the front of my hips. With his heavy weight pressing into me, I finally drift back to sleep.

"Merow."

I blink my eyes open and barely stop myself from jumping backward when I realize that we're nose to nose. I slide my cell phone from the bedside table without breaking eye contact with the massive cat that I'm locked eyes with and check the time.

"Merow," he complains.

I'm sure he's hungry. It's somewhere between late morning and early afternoon.

"All right, handsome," I coo as I scratch under his chin. "Let's get you something to eat."

I toss back the covers and kick my legs over the side of the bed, leaving my phone mixed into the sheets. He follows me as I pad to the kitchen. I dump the bowl of dry food in the trash and toss the bowl in the sink. I pull a clean one down from the cabinet and fill it with fresh kibble while he looks on with disdain. I swear it's like having Gordon Ramsey in a cat body.

I set the bowl on the floor and do the same with his water dish all while Bogey sits there watching me, looking supremely unimpressed.

"Merow," he complains.

I roll my eyes and let out a puff of air. "Fine."

He can be such a brat sometimes and yet he's the only one that's stood by me through the last few weeks. I guess being my only ride or die deserves a special treat. So I pull another little cat bowl from the cupboard and open a can of tuna. I spoon a little bit into one side of the bowl and then pop a cover on top of the can to save the rest when, really, we know that it will fester and die, forgotten.

I drop it on a shelf of the fridge to begin its fruitless endeavor to become a cure for cancer or venereal disease and grab a bag of mini cubes of cheese.

I check the expiration date and give the contents a sniff. No signs of mold or other fungus so it's probably still good. I pop one into my mouth and all is well, so I sprinkle a couple on the other side of the bowl.

Fuck me, I just made my cat a charcuterie board.

I shrug to myself and place the bowl on the

floor. Bogey jumps on it with glee in his hazel kitty eyes.

"Thanks for always being my guy," I tell him as I stroke his back while he annihilates the contents of his special dinner.

I guess I should consider what to feed myself for the day. While I'm not sick, I don't feel good. My body feels off and my heart feels weak. I'm not sure how many more emotional blows I can take and, when I feel like this, I want comfort.

To me, comfort is Mrs. Yee's hot and sour soup but I'm not ready to see how disappointed in me they will be when they find out how badly I blew it with Hunter. They were so happy to welcome him to the family.

Maybe I can make my own … or maybe pigs can fly. Either way, I need to leave this apartment to find sustenance.

I make my way back into my bedroom and pull on a pair of leggings and an oversized shirt with the University of Buffalo logo cracked and peeling off in places because it's been so well worn. I slide my feet into a pair of running shoes and twist my hair up in a messy bun before heading out. I grab my bag on the way and make sure that the door locks behind me.

I take the stairs a little faster than normal. Maybe if I get my heart pumping it won't hurt as much. I'm just going to add this one to the long list of lies

I tell myself to try and make me feel better about something … everything. Honestly, who knows at this point.

I push open the front door and blink against the bright sun. Outside feels so bright and shiny and happy and I'm honestly not here for that shit so I pull a pair of oversized sunglasses from my bag and toss them on my face. I walk toward the bodega a couple blocks down.

Maybe I can make my own soup, poor Mrs. Yee has tried to show me enough times. But then again, I'd probably burn down my building in the process, get rescued by a hot fireman, who would cause me all kinds of emotional distress. Because somewhere along the way, I decided that Hunter was mine and I was his, even if he was maybe a cold blooded killer because I went and caught feelings.

Stupid, lousy feelings that he made me feel when I definitely didn't want to. And now he's gone. Lost to me forever and I'm all alone.

I pass the bodega and walk another block to the little Chinese place that is not my family restaurant where I feel comfortable and loved, but they do have a great hot and sour soup. Bonus points, because no one knows me here so no one will pry into my dismal love life.

I order a large soup, spring rolls, and shrimp fried rice, handing the hostess my credit card that she swipes quickly before handing it back to me with the receipt. I'm not even sure that she looked at me in the process, which I am totally okay with because I haven't even processed the way my life swirled down the toilet on my own yet, let alone with other people.

Moments later someone from the back comes out with an oversized, brown paper lunch sack. She takes it from him and hands it to me with a quick, "Come again."

"Thanks," I reply. "I will."

I carefully arrange the bag in my tote bag and start walking home. As I near my building, I have that weird feeling that someone is watching me, but a quick look around the area shows no one is there. Sadness swells in my heart when I realize it's probably Hunter. He claimed me, he must be feeling as drawn to me as I am to him. And I bet he fucking hates that.

I type in the code and pull open the door. I still feel my Spidey senses tingling so I take the stairs two at a time and then realize that this is how the girl always dies in the horror movies. Alone in a freaking stairwell with an axe murderer. Jesus, I'm an idiot.

By some miracle, I manage to get my keys out without fumbling them and let myself into the apartment. I quickly lock the door behind me and set the chain and the deadbolt. A single girl living alone in the city can't be too careful, especially when her gut is telling her that danger is close.

I take a deep breath and roll my shoulders back before marching into the kitchen. I set my tote bag on the counter and pull out the bag of food. My tote is going to smell like fried spring rolls for days and I can't find myself all broken up about it.

I set the soup in the fridge thinking it'll reheat well later tonight and take the spring rolls and the rice containers to the living room. I kick off my sneakers and head back to the kitchen for chopsticks and a can of coke. When I have everything I need, I head back to the living room and settle in.

I pop open the soda and set it on the table next to me before picking up the remote and scrolling through. I land on Hallmark. Maybe all the sweet love stories will be like ripping off a Band-Aid.

I pull the chenille throw from the back of the sofa and toss it over my legs. Even though the weather is still warm, I love snuggly blankets. I even keep fans running during the summer so I can cuddle in. I open the paper bucket of fried rice and dig in.

Bogey magically materializes at my feet and hurls his hefty body up onto the sofa next to me with a "Merow." It's like being slapped with a walrus.

"Hey buddy," I greet him and then offer him a little bite of shrimp off of the end of my chopsticks.

He gobbles it up greedily. I am well aware that this is part of why he's a little chonky. It's also part of why I am a little chonky.

We sit back and share the rice. He has no interest in veggie spring rolls, so those are mine alone. Eventually, the movie ends and another one starts. Jesse Metcalf is a country singer with an awful fiancé. I'm here for that. I take the rest of the rice to the kitchen and stuff it in the fridge for dinner.

Sometime before Jesse gets the real girl of his dreams, I fall asleep on the sofa with Bogey in my arms.

Naked. I am naked and in a large bathtub. The steam from the water rises up and fills the room as the tub slowly fills around me. The sound of the water running relaxes me after a difficult night at home. The anger that fills me when I think about my husband and how he doesn't appreciate me anymore. All I ever wanted was for Randall to love me. To want me. But I guess I was asking too much.

The door clicks as the knob turns from the outside and the door is pushed open. I wonder if maybe I finally got through to Randall and he decided to surprise me now, in the middle of the day.

But when the door opens completely, it doesn't reveal Randall, but someone else entirely, someone

*who knows me more intimately than Randall. I'm
sad that my husband doesn't want me like he used
to but this one does and I've decided to grab hold
of the opportunity. Maybe this is my second chance
at happiness.*

"Hey," he says with a smile on his face.

*"Hi," I reply. "I didn't expect to see you to-
day."*

*"I just couldn't stay away," he says as he pulls
his polo shirt up over his head and drops it to the
counter.*

*"Is that so?" I ask as I snuggle down into the
warm water, hoping he likes what he sees as much
as I know he does.*

*"Absolutely." he drops to his knees next to the
tub and reaches into the water with a strong hand,
dropping it instantly between my spread thighs.*

*He toys with me, his fingers moving over me
before thrusting two deep inside, making me gasp.*

*"Mmm," I purr as he takes me higher but then,
without warning, he withdraws his fingers from my
core and I snap my eyes open. "What are you doing?"*

*"I'm sorry, Sarah," he says as he pushes up to
stand over me.*

*I move to cover my nudity with my hands but
what I should have done was ward off an attack.
Feeling humiliated that now not one, but two men
in my life want nothing to do with me, I just want to*

curl up and hide.

I never see him coming.

Before I know it, his hand wraps around my neck and squeezes. I gasp for air and I'm sure confusion glitters in my eyes. He doesn't seem confused at all as he pushes me under the water.

I pull and scratch at his hands and arms but it's no use. He won't let me go.

My lungs burn. I can't hold my breath any longer.

Bubbles pop out of my mouth as the air rushes out and the water rushes in. And then I let go and everything just ... fades away into nothingness.

I gasp as I come awake, the burn of the water filling my lungs is still with me as I sit up on the couch.

Bogeyis long gone. Where, I don't know but he's never far. Perhaps he's on the fire escape singing to the female across the alley.

I get up and pace my apartment. I hate these dreams and I hate that they're still coming. I just want them to stop. The worst part is the one that Hunter plays in them as my deadly lover. I know now that he was no killer even though it's too late to salvage our relationship. And I hate that he's still in the spot of the real killer. If only my dreams would show me who it really is, maybe we could all move on.

Hunter and Brody could close their case. Sure,

I'll see Brody from time to time—he is dating my best friend. That is, if she even wants the job. But Hunter and I are done. I know that now. But maybe, once everything is said and done, my family will be able to finally move on from that dream. It's clear that the Jones curse is still alive and well.

I feel dirty. Unclean. I need a shower. I make my way into my bathroom and start the water. I hate that the memory of Hunter and I in this space is so fresh, so close to the surface. Even though we were only together for a short time, it's clear that it's going to take quite a while to exorcise him from my life.

I strip off my clothes and step into the hot water and steam and make quick work of scrubbing every inch of my body until it's pink and slightly abraded. I shut off the water and dry my skin with a towel before combing out my long hair and braiding it down my back to dry in beachy waves for tomorrow.

I head into my bedroom and pull on stripped drawstring shorts with lace trim in blue and white and a matching lace trim cami in the same blue. I top it with an old college sweatshirt of a boyfriend from long since past.

I head back into the main part of the apartment and into the kitchen. It's well past five in the evening, and you know what Jimmy Buffet says, so I pull a bottle of wine out of the fridge and unearth a bottle opener from the junk drawer. I pour myself a huge glass while I heat up the leftover rice and soup.

Instead of heading back to the sofa, I eat standing at the counter. Afterward, I throw away the empty containers and pour myself another glass of wine that I drink while loading the dishwasher. Feeling sleepy and still a little melancholy, I decide to head to bed early.

I brush my teeth and then shut off the lights in the rest of the apartment. It seems pointless, but I try to straighten the rumpled covers before climbing in and pulling the blankets up to my chin. I'm not sure that I'll be able to settle in at all and prepare myself for a long, restless night.

Instead, sleep claims me quickly and I never once notice that my phone is nowhere to be found. Not that it matters anyway, because no one calls me.

26

I don't want you

The sheets whisper down my body. This dream is so much better than the one where I die. Strong hands roll me to my back, but I don't open my eyes. I know exactly who it is and if I can only have him in my dreams, then I'll take it.

I feel the front of my cami pull down freeing my breasts just before his tongue swipes the tip of my nipple. I arch into him, offering more of me, ready for him to devour me if he wishes, and he rewards me with a growl around my hard tip that I feel between my legs.

I whimper as he lets me go but he doesn't go far. He slides his hand up the leg of my sleep shorts and swipes a finger through my center. I know what he finds there; I'm wet and wanting. I need him with a ferocity that can bring us both to our knees.

I ruined the reality, but here in my dreams, it's ours for the taking.

He plunges a finger deep inside me while he presses the pad of his thumb down on my clit. My breathing picks up as he pumps his digit in and out of me, finding that spot that makes my toes curl. He adds another finger and then another until the stretch to fit him inside me burns as he gives me no time to adjust.

I don't care.

I want it. I'll do anything for it, but what I don't do is open my eyes.

Instead, I clench them tight because I know that when I open them, it'll all be over. I'll wake up and Hunter will be gone.

He pushes me harder and faster until my climax barrels through me and I come with a scream. But he doesn't do is kiss me. Never once do his lips touch mine, be it tender or rough. And I'm too far gone in his sexual haze to realize that something is oh-so very wrong. Once again, he gives me no time, whipping my cami over my head and my shorts down my legs, leaving me bare for him.

Only for him.

And then he flips me to my belly. He kicks my knees up underneath me and pushes them wide.

I know that I'm going to feel him inside me

again and I can't wait. If I had known that the last time would be the last for real, I would have cherished it. Reveled in it and made it last, drawing our passions out for as long as he would let me.

He pushes my chest to the bed, holding me down when I want to rise up to meet him. I feel the blunt head of his cock at my opening. But it's when he drives in deep—harder and faster than I can take, a searing burn as my body is forced to stretch around him—that my eyes pop open and my head flies back.

This is not a dream.

Hunter grabs my braid in his fist as he pumps in and out of me, pulling me up to balance on my knees.

I drop my hands to the headboard for balance as he continues to drive into me with a savage pace. And even though he's harsher than normal, I want him. My body reacts to him as my nipples pebble harder and my pussy floods for him.

One hand holds me firmly, the pads of his fingers digging into my hip as he holds me still to take his fucking. But it's the other that he tenderly skates up my body and wraps around my breast, plucking my nipple that has me bucking against him.

And then he slides it down to where we're joined, feeling the savage beauty of his cock plunging deep inside of me.

"I fucking love this," he growls against the side

of my neck as he pulls my hair tighter. The sting against my scalp only drives me higher.

"Yes," I pant.

"I fucking love the feel of your hot cunt as it grips my cock."

"Yes, yes."

"And I fucking love how wet you are," he says as he moves his fingers to my clit to pluck and pinch my most sensitive parts as he forces me closer and closer to another climax. "How you gush for me."

"Yes." I dig my nails into the headboard, grasping for purchase on anything to keep me standing as Hunter pushes my body to new heights.

"And I love the way your pussy grips my cock when you come," he growls, pumping his hips into me over and over. "Do it."

"Hunter," I gasp. I don't think I can take it anymore. If I let this orgasm go it won't roll over me gently, it'll wreck me.

"Do it now," he orders. "Fucking come."

"Oh God," I pant and keen.

"God won't help you now," he rumbles. "Let. Fucking. Go."

And then it crashes into me like grabbing a live wire. I'm helpless to stop it as I keen and cry out, every muscle in my body shaking and Hunter has to hold me up.

"Fuck yes," he rumbles as he pushes me to the mattress and follows me down. I feel his hard chest against my back as he plunges into me again and again.

His hold on my braid tightens as he pulls, tipping my head to the side for his strike. This is unlike any claiming bite he has given me before. This hurts. The pain burns through me like a wildfire, and I gasp against it. But Hunter doesn't care, or maybe it only drives him higher, because he plants his cock deep inside me and comes.

He pulls my hair, tipping me further as he trails his nose up the column of my neck, taking in the scent of me, of us, and his claiming. "But you know what I hate?" he snarls.

I don't want to answer him, I really don't. Things are becoming more and more clear. Hunter is here, not to love but to punish me.

It's like a car crash and I can't help but look when I answer him softly. "What?"

"I hate that I want you so much," he growls. "I hate that I need you the way I do."

"Hunter," I gasp. "Please."

"I don't want you … Or, I don't want to want you," he says as he pulls out of me quickly, letting his hold on me go at the same time.

I turn my head and watch as he stands. He didn't even take off his jeans or boots before joining me. Only his chest is bare. He looks me dead in the eyes as he tucks his softening cock back in his jeans. As he buttons them up, he says, "I don't want you at all."

I don't open my mouth to say anything. What could I say, anyway? He was pretty clear on his wants and wishes. I don't answer him. I just watch with rapt attention as he tags his t-shirt from the end of the bed and storms out of my room like the hounds of hell are on his heels. Again.

I lay there, naked in my bed, his cum leaking out of me. My body so thoroughly used, and not in the good ways he's made me feel before. Now I'm sore and aching but it's nothing compared to the breath stopping pain in my chest.

"Please, just let me go," I whisper in a sob. I try to muffle it as best as I can, but I know that he hears it when there's a pause between the front door opening and when it slams closed behind him. "Just let me go."

Now I know that even though he doesn't want me, he's going to continue to come to me, to use me in the night, and I'm going to have to be the one to put a stop to it.

It's going to kill me to send him away. But this? This is unbearable.

27
Done

Sleep didn't come quickly or softly. I guess the sandman wasn't feeling very merciful with me last night.

Instead, I laid awake for hours feeling raw and flayed open. I slept rough, off and on, never really getting a break from the earth titling pain in my heart.

Is it possible to stop breathing and still be alive? At some point, I think I stopped living and began just existing. There's no possible way someone can live with the amount of pain Hunter inflicted.

Why couldn't he just leave me alone? Why wouldn't Hunter let me be? Does he really hate me that much?

I cringe as Taylor cockily croons about bad

breakups. I was cocky, too, the other night. I felt like I had done nothing wrong but feeling the way that I do this morning, I can't help but wonder if maybe I did.

I lean over and I reach for my phone on the night stand to silence my alarm but it's not there. I have to dig around for it and fling myself to hang over the side of the bed to find it underneath. I swipe it from it's hiding place and I sit, staring at the home screen for a bit, before I work up the courage to do what needs to be done. I made a mistake, and I'm human so I'm going to from time to time, but I can also own up to it. And I will, but that doesn't give Hunter the right to use me and discard me so cruelly either.

I pull up our text thread and come face to face with the reminder that we've been nothing but toxic the entire time. I can't help but feel like fated mates should be a little nicer to each other than we've been. No wonder there's no trust between us.

I take a deep breath and find the courage to do what needs to be done.

ME: I messed up.

ME: I should have known that you weren't a killer and for that, I'm truly sorry.

Little dots appear, showing that he's reading the message and typing a reply. I can't let him do that. Any contact with him and I'll fold like a lawn chair. I'm so weak where he's concerned. So I type out the rest as fast as I can.

> ME: But you hurt me. We can't go on like this. You hurting me and then me hurting you or vice versa. This isn't healthy and we both deserve better.

> ME: So, for my part in anything that caused you pain, I am sorry. More so than you will ever know. But I'm also done. I can't keep letting you in to hurt me again.

> ME: So please don't call me. Don't come to my work or my apartment. I need to find my balance again and to do that I need space.

And then I quickly tap his name at the top of the message and thumb over to his contact page and hit BLOCK. It hurts, the knowledge that I'll not have him in my life in any way. But it also feels like a huge weight has been lifted off my shoulders because I was never going to make Hunter happy. Twisting myself into knots to try would never work, but it's also wrong.

I toss the covers back and slide my legs over the side, climbing out of bed. Even though I showered last night, I feel dirty after the way Hunter handled me. I need to wash. I need to be clean. I make my way into the bathroom and run the water as hot as I can stand it, but I strip down and climb in before the temperature rises. I let the icy water sting and then soothe as it heats up before I grab my loofa and scrub myself until I'm practically raw.

I grab a towel and dry off. I put more makeup on my face than I usually do to try and hide the bags under my eyes, but it's no use. I look like hammered horse shit. I unbraid my hair from last night and let it fall around my shoulders in beachy waves, pinning just the very front back away from my face.

I hang up my towel and walk naked through my apartment back to my room. I pull on my bra and panties and then my most comfortable pair of jeggings, they're more legging than jean but so comfy, and a loose fitting bat-wing blouse. I slide my feet into a pair of converse sneakers and grab my bag on my way out the door.

I don't stop for breakfast, instead, I drive straight to the school and park in the parking lot. And again, I feel like someone is watching me as I walk through the front gates. And once again, I look around but see nothing.

It makes me angry. Why won't Hunter just leave me alone? This is ridiculous.

He made it abundantly clear that he hates me, so why continue to make me feel uncomfortable everywhere I go? Well I'm not going to give him anymore of my time or attention! I am done.

I walk straight through the school and to the faculty lounge. I make a pot of coffee and as soon as it brews, I pour myself a huge mug, carrying it with me to my classroom. I unlock the door and push it open, pausing as I see the light under Amanda's door is still dark. Maybe she's out again. My heart pangs at the thought that we haven't talked in a few days. I hate it.

I set my coffee and my tote bag on my desk before pulling the chairs down from on top of the kids' tables. I set my classroom to rights and before I know it, the coffee is gone and the kids are beginning to arrive.

"yetis the handsome policeman a good kisser, Miss Jones?" Emily, one of my students asks when she raises her hand during circle time. Jesus fucking Christ. Not this again.

"Uhh…" I start and feel like maybe I'm having a stroke. Thirty is too young for a stroke, right? Why would a four year old ask if someone is a good kisser? What kind of shit is she watching at home. Granted this is the kid who gets dropped off in a Mercedes by a nanny and yesterday shared she got a new iphone over the weekend. So my guess is anything she fucking wants.

"Of course he's a good kissser, dummy," another student answers. "He's a policeman. He has a badge and a gun."

"Did you see that gun?" Timmy adds and I wonder if I'm stuck in some time loop. This is ridiculous.

"We are not having another class discussion about a gun and that's final," I snap.

I'm answered with a chorus of "Sorry, Miss Jones." Again. I really wish these kids would let the idea of Hunter and me go. They're about as bad as my family.

"But you did kiss him, right?" Emily asks and man, that kid is like a dog with a bone.

"Of course she did, dummy."

"Kids—" I start.

"I'm not a dummy. You're a dummy." Jesus H. It never ends.

"Kids—" I try again but am cut off by the bell for recess, Thank you God. "Line up and we'll head out to recess." Just another day teaching four and five year olds…

In a more organized manner than they would throughout the rest of the day, my class gets in their lines in order. I grab the cup of coffee off my desk and count them off by their class number and when I'm sure we haven't forgotten someone in the bathroom, I lead them through the halls and out to the blacktop.

When they hit the playground, they scatter to the wind. I take my coffee and wander over to the other side of the playground by the handball courts to supervise the kids. It's my new spot that I've claimed since my life imploded and I'm still trying to find my way. I knew hitting thirty would be rough, but I didn't think it would be this rough.

I take a sip of my now cooler coffee and wonder if there's any salvaging my relationships, not with Hunter, but with everyone else.

Amanda slides in beside me and bumps her hip to mine.

I hold my breath, wondering what she's going to say next, and I realize that I missed her even more than I thought I did.

"Hey," she says softly, and I can't help but wonder if she's gauging my reaction like I am hers.

"Hey back." We stand next to each other, both vacantly watching the kids as they run and play for quite a bit before she breaks the silence.

"So you're a powerful witch?" she whispers and I laugh.

"Not even a little bit."

"So your family is powerful?" she clarifies.

"Yes," I answer. "But if you're worried about someone turning you into a toad because you hurt my feelings then don't be. That's not how we roll."

"Well, obviously." she laughs. "Or else I would have been a toad since freshman year when I went out with Derek Chambers not knowing he called you a cow in the commons and said he'd never date you."

"Yeah." I laugh as we stroll down memory lane. "But you more than made up for it when you told everyone you never should have gone out with him and his tiny penis."

"I know, right?" she laughs.

"I particularly enjoyed the part about how I dodged his needle-dick bullet," I add.

"Me too. It was one of my better moments," she says before pausing in thought for a moment. "I'm sorry."

"Me too."

"No," she says firmly and for a split second I wonder if she's going to tell me that we can't be friends anymore. That would be awful. "I'm really sorry. I was an awful cow."

"You're not an awful cow."

"I was and you were just trying to tell me this big huge secret that had nothing to do with me and I was awful and selfish and made it all about me and I'm really, really sorry."

"It's okay," I tell her, wrapping my arm around her. She tips her head to my shoulder. "All is forgiven."

"Can we still be friends?" she asks me.

"We never weren't."

"Thank you," she whispers.

"So… you and Brody," I whisper back.

"Yeah," she replies and this time I can hear the smile in her voice. "Me and Brody. So you and

Hunter?"

My heart clenches at her gentle question. "Not so much."

Amanda picks her head up and turns to look at me. "What?" she asks. "I don't understand."

"We're no good for each other," I explain.

"But … that's not how Brody said mates work," She says. "I don't know. It's all new to me. I mean, I didn't even know you were a witch and I've known you forever."

"I know," I reply and feel like someone sucked all the air out of my lungs. "I guess we weren't true mates after all."

"But …" she starts.

"But what?" I ask.

"I don't know if I should tell you," she replies.

"It's okay, Amanda," I tell her gently. "I'm a big girl and I can take whatever you want to share with me and whatever you don't because I'm your friend. Okay?"

"Okay."

"See?" I ask. "It'll be all right."

"Hunter is the one who told Brody to tell me to talk to you," she blurts out and hearing his name on her lips slices open a wound on my heart that will never heal. Instead, it will fester and rot until it's ripped open all over again. "Hunter told him how much it was hurting you that I was so angry and that he didn't like it. He was right, you know? I was too hard on you."

"Well, all is forgiven," I whisper.

"It's just that …"

"It's just what?" I whisper.

"It's just that Brody said that Hunter's bossiness was a mix of his alpha tendencies mixed with his protective nature over his fated mate."

"Well, then you have nothing to worry about," I say, forcing a smile. "I'm not his fated mate and we've mended fences, so all is well."

"I guess so …"

"I know so," I reply. "Besides, I don't know anything about alpha tendencies, but he is bossy. Too bossy for me."

"I heard you liked him bossy against your mom's garage," she says, and I gasp in mock outrage.

"Shame on you!" I laugh. "I can't believe you said that."

"It was funny though."

"And true," I sigh. "But it is what it is."

"What happened?" she asks gently.

"We didn't trust each other. I didn't trust him, and he's hurt so he hurt me," I explain. "We've become too toxic and now there's no fixing things. I ended it this morning."

"What did Hunter say to that?"

"I don't know. I blocked him."

"What?" she laughs. "Ohmygod. Girl, you're

in so much trouble."

"No, I'm not," I reply, rolling my eyes. "I bet he doesn't even care."

"We'll see," she says.

"Yes, we will, and I'll be the one saying I told you so."

"Fine," she says. "But I don't think you need to sit at home and wallow tonight. Come out for drinks and bar dinner with Brody and me."

"I don't want to be a third wheel."

"You're not a third wheel," she says, and I side eye her. "We are capable of keeping our hands off of each other for the span of a dinner."

"If you say so."

"I do," she replies smugly. "So, Homerun at seven?"

"Sure," I agree.

Famous last words, right?

28

Keep 'em coming

What am I even doing here?

I park my car in the lot behind the bar and shut off the engine. I contemplate banging my head against the steering wheel until maybe my life makes more sense but that seems a little too dramatic, even for me.

So with a heavy sigh on my lips, I pull my keys from the ignition and grab my tote bag from the passenger seat. I shut the car door behind me and beep the locks before making my way around the building.

The hair stands up on the back of my neck and that feeling of being watched sends shivers down my spine. I look over my shoulder as I hurry through the parking lot but find nothing out of place. I feel my face flush hot with anger and frustration. Damn that man!

"Leave me alone, Hunter," I say lower than a whisper. I know that if he's out here like I think he is, he'll hear me with his supervillain hearing. Maybe one day he'll even get the message and end the romantic warfare.

Ten minutes ago, I didn't even want to be here, in this bar, playing pickup games of does he like me or does he not with strangers. But now, a petty part of me that I'm not proud of wants him to see that I'm not the worthless garbage he's decided that I am. It would do good for him to see someone else want me.

Like I said, I'm not proud. I'm hurt and hurt people do stupid shit. I can let a stranger buy me a drink, right? Although, the thought of it burns through my gut like stale coffee and my heart pangs in my chest. It wants no one but Hunter.

I push through the glass-fronted door and see Amanda sitting on a stool at the bar. Brody is standing beside her and they're so wrapped up in each other it's like they're the only ones in the world, not just the bar.

A sharp pain sears through my chest. Jealousy, I guess. I won't ever have that. As long as Hunter has a claim on me, I'll never have someone so wrapped up in me that they don't know where they end and I begin.

I should go.

I should turn around before they see me and walk away. Head home and text Amanda that I just wasn't up to it tonight. Not only for my sake, but hers as well. She and Brody don't need to babysit me and my broken heart. They should be blissfully ensconced in the love bubble.

That's what I'll do. I'll go home and put on some comfy pajamas and make some scrambled eggs and toast and wallow a bit. Nothing helps heal the heart like comfort food and a Netflix binge. I turn to walk back out the door when I hear someone call my name.

"Penelope!" Brody's voice rings out over the noise of the bar. I turn to look back at them and think I see someone familiar, but they're gone when I turn back. "Over here!"

"Damn," I mutter under my breath. I've been spotted. I try to think of an excuse to go. Possibilities swirl around in my brain as I make my way through the after-work crush of people toward my friends.

"Hey," Amanda greets me with a smile. "Long time, no see."

"Hey, back," I laugh.

"Good to see you, Penelope," Brody says.

I look to him to gauge the sincerity of his words. I find only honesty and truth on his face.

"Good to see you too," I reply.

"What will you have?" he asks me as he raises his hand to flag down the bartender.

"I don't know," I say before rolling my lip in between my teeth and then letting it go with a pop. "I'm not feeling so hot. I think maybe I should just call it a night."

"No!" Amanda shouts a little too quickly. "You just got here."

"I know but I'm not sure I'm ready yet."

"Just one drink," she pleads with her puppy dog eyes.

"Fine," I capitulate as I roll my eyes.

"Yay!"

"A white wine please."

"Nooo. That's boring," she says. "And no way to nurse a broken heart. You need whiskey."

I chance an awkward glance at Brody to see his reaction to her announcement of my inception to the broken heart's club. He just smiles gently at me as if it's old news. I guess I shouldn't be surprised. I forgot what it's like to be part of a couple that shares everything with each other.

I roll my shoulders back and pull in a steadying breath before turning to the bartender. "I guess whiskey it is. Can I have a Jack and Coke please?"

"Coming right up," he says with a wink. He's young and cute and has a flirty vibe to him and if I cared at all, I would flirt right back.

But alas, my heart's just not into it. My heart's

just not into him. It wants Hunter, the one man who will never want me back and I have no one to blame but myself. I should have talked to him. I should have told him about my dreams and my fears sooner before it all blew up in my face. Maybe we could have worked it out. But now we'll never know.

The bartender sets my drink on the bar in front of me and I hang my bag off the back of the barstool before climbing up. I place my palms on the battered wood top and lean in to take the mini straw in between my lips and suck back some much needed whiskey.

I let the smoky flavors of the whiskey and the crisp bubbles of the soda pop over my tongue and warm me up from the inside out, mellowing me as it moves along. I take another deep breath and relax into my bar stool before turning to face Brody and Amanda.

Brody stands close to her, their arms wrapped around each other as they study me.

Well, shit. I was hoping that I could avoid the elephant in the room for as long as possible—maybe even forever—but it looks as if the lovebirds aren't going to let anything slide tonight.

"So …" I start. "What's new?"

"I could ask the same of you," Brody answers.

"Hmm …" I twirl my straw in my mouth and pull some whiskey back.

"So," he starts.

"Babe—" Amanda tries to interrupt but it's no use.

"What the fuck is going on?" he asks. His voice is low and bristling with anger.

"I'm sorry," I whisper. "Maybe I should go."

"Brody," Amanda warns. "Enough."

"I didn't say you had to go, but babe, what the fuck is going on?"

I push out a heavy breath and then answer. "Nothing is going on."

"Now, what's the truth?"

"That is the truth," I reply and when he gives me a look that says he's not sure he believes me, I push on. "It's true. We had a thing and I messed it up. Then he messed it up worse and now we're nothing."

"Nothing," he repeats like he's testing the word. He watches me as he mulls it over.

"Yes."

"Okay."

"Okay," I repeat and when he opens his mouth to ask me something else, I jump in. "Can we just let it all go for tonight? I just really need to forget tonight."

"Okay, babe," he says softly, and I watch Amanda's body melt against him. Her body language belying how stressed out she was, worrying about a confrontation between me and her man. She must really want to move on and put this fight behind us and I'm grateful for the opportunity to have my friend back. "We can let it go. For now."

"Thanks."

"Bartender!" I call out.

"What can I do for you, beautiful?" he answers. His double meaning is clear.

I shake my almost empty glass. "Keep 'em coming!"

"Sure thing," he winks.

He places another drink in front of me and collects my empty glass while Amanda and I make small talk about nothing and everything. And then the song changes and she leaps up.

"Ohmygod! I love this song!" she squeals, making me smile as only she can. My bestie is full of life. She tempers my moodiness.

"Go," I say. I give her a nudge, knowing she's trying to temper her night to match my mood but it's not what she should do. I don't ever want the people I love to change who they are for me. I wouldn't want them to want me to be less of who I am for them. "I think you need to dance to your favorite song."

"Come with?" she asks.

"No," I reply with a smile so her feelings aren't hurt. "But I can think of someone else who'd like to dance with you."

"Are you sure?"

"Absolutely."

Brody holds his hand out to her, and she takes it, placing her slim hand in his upturned one and hopping down from her stool. He watches me from over his shoulder before letting her lead him away with a smirk playing about on his handsome mouth. I like him for her. They balance each other out and complement each other in ways that lovers should.

I turn back to play with the stray in my glass and let my mind wander over all of the ways that Hunter and I did *not* complement each other like that. I'm a rip the Band-Aid off fast kind of a girl. I could sit and stew and let the wound fester for weeks and weeks. Or I could accept what was, what isn't meant for me, and I can find the courage to look for ways to be happy with the life that I'm meant to lead. Alone.

I'll be all right. Really, I will.

In the grand scheme of things, Hunter and I didn't really know each other all that long. And for most of it, I thought he was capable of murder. That's not long enough to be feeling as low as I do right now. We burned too hot and too fast like some candles do while others are slower to ignite, but can burn for what seems like eternity. That all-consuming heat can't be sustained for long and I would do well to remember that in the future.

Now I just need to focus on how I'm going to move on with my life. Mom and Grandma will have to get over it eventually. I'm not going to lie, their silence feels a lot like they chose Hunter in the break-up. Which is utterly ridiculous because they've both lived through the Jones family curse. They know first-hand that true love is not meant for us. Only heartache and devastation.

Until they forgive me, I'll have my class and Bogey.

Bogey is the only soul who has never wavered from his loyalty to me. I could not imagine my life, no matter what path I were on, without that big hairy meatball of a cat. I'm so thankful for his companionship. I'm ready to be a crazy cat lady. So much so that I can't believe I ever considered any other life goal.

Speaking of my class, I am going to have to figure out what to do about Mr. Simmons. I hate the looks that I keep getting from Mrs. Simmons. I don't deserve them, and I won't ever do what she thinks I have. I'm not that kind of woman.

Besides, all that stress can't be good for either her or the baby.

But I can't let Mr. Simmons keep flirting with me like he does. It makes me uncomfortable and I need his advances to stop. I'm going to have to talk to Marcie about it, even if it means I no longer get to have Timmy in my class. It will be better this way in the long run.

I'm so lost in my thoughts that I don't realize that my glass is empty again. The bartender sets another glass in front of me, replacing the old one.

"Thanks," I whisper.

He smiles and nods at something behind me. "It's from the man across the room."

But when I look over my shoulder, there's no one there. I mean the room is full of the usual after-work crowd, but there's no one I recognize. No one who looks like they sent a drink to a woman they don't know.

Weird.

"Well, thank you from me."

I feel the hair on the back of my neck stand on end like someone is watching me. I know in my gut that someone is here. I can feel the menace swirling in the room around me. I swivel on my barstool one more time to take a look around and see Hunter striding through the people on the dance floor to reach the spot where Brody has Amanda in his arms.

A woman stops him in his tracks, halfway to his goal, with her slim hand on his forearm. I watch like someone on the interstate would drive past a car wreck as Hunter turns to her with a brilliant smile on his face. He's so handsome with his face soft and happy.

I'm not sure that I've ever seen him look at me that way, but it seems to come easy to him now. And who could blame him.

She's beautiful with dark, glossy hair that falls

around her shoulders in loose waves, drawing attention to her full breasts. Her red lips are turned up in invitation as she smiles a woman's smile at him and her eyes sparkle with a promise of what's to come.

I know that feeling well, and I know enough about myself to know that I can't stay here and watch their night unfold, leading them, no doubt, to the bedroom and beyond.

It was stupid of me to think that he deserved to see me with someone else, that maybe knowing I was worth it would force him to eat a little crow. Because now that the shoe is on the other foot, it's not funny at all. It fucking hurts.

I can't stay here. I turn back to my drink. My head is pounding, and I feel sick to my stomach. Seeing Hunter in the arms of another woman is killing me. If this is what having a mate is like, then I don't want it. It's awful.

I sling my tote bag around from the back of my chair and drop it in my lap. I flip it open and root around for my wallet. Fortunately, I carry a giant grandma wallet with an old school checkbook and check register in it because when you're living on a kindergarten teacher's salary you have to watch every penny. Especially when you have a love for takeaway like I do.

I drop a bunch of bills on the bar top, much more than is needed but I don't have time to wait for the check. I don't want Hunter to see me sneaking out, or worse, be spotted by Amanda or Brody. No doubt they might make me stay and watch the awkward mating dance between my former lover and his new flame. Not to mention, the bartender gave good flirt and made me feel pretty if only for a moment. It was a nice moment, at that.

I toss my wallet back into my tote bag and sling it over my shoulder as I hop down from the bar stool. It spins with my hasty exit, but I don't stop to steady it.

Instead, I push my way through the growing crowd toward the restrooms in the back. I figure I can sneak out the staff entrance and call an Uber. I've had too much to drink to try and drive home and it's much too late to walk. Monsters of all kinds come out in the dark.

I step into the long hall at the back of the bar when someone grabs me from behind. Strong hands that feel all wrong turn me around and my stomach pitches. Something is really wrong. I look up into the blue eyes of my student's dad.

"Mr. Simmons?" I ask. I blink my eyes several times to try to clear them. I must be seeing things.

"I told you to call me Bill," he smiles.

"I think I should be going," I tell him. "I'm not feeling so well."

"Not so fast," he replies and then he crushes his mouth to mine and forces his tongue between my lips.

"What are you doing?" I gasp when I push him back, managing to get a little bit of space between us. I don't want this. I've never wanted this.

"What I should have done all along, Penelope," he says as his arms pull my body into his.

He kisses me again and, again, I try to push him away.

"No!"

I feel his erection pressing against my hip and I want to throw up.

"Why are you fighting me?" he asks as he grips my breast hard. I feel tears sting the backs of my eyes. "I know that you want this."

"No," I plead. "No, I don't."

The room is spinning. I shouldn't have drunk so much. I shouldn't have sent my friends off. I should have stayed where I was. I was so naïve to think that I would be safe at the bar in my neighborhood. I was never safe at all.

"I don't think you're really in a position to argue," he tells me as he hoists me up over his shoulder like a sack of potatoes.

The sad thing is he's right because everything goes black.

29

Superman jammies

TIMMY

"Bill, please," Mommy cries. "Please don't go."

Mommy is always crying.

"Stop it, Brenda," Daddy yells.

I pull the blankets up over my head as the front door opens and closes.

Mommy cries even louder.

I hear footsteps outside my bedroom door and I squeeze my eyes closed and pretend like I'm sleeping. I know not to be awake when Mommy is sad. She's not mean, just … weird. I don't like it. It makes me feel funny.

My door swings open and I hear her walk to my bed. She pulls the blankets down so they don't cover my face any more and I hold really, really still. Mommy brushes my hair back from my face and places a wet kiss to my cheek.

"Don't worry, baby," she whispers with a sniffle. "Mommy's going to make it all okay. Mommy's going to fix our little family." And then she leaves my room and shuts the door behind her all quiet like.

The front door opens and then closes and her car starts up and drives away! My mommy left me! But that can't be right. Mommies don't leave their little children all alone, do they?

I sit up and look at the alarm clock on the table next to my bed. I don't know what the numbers mean but Mommy always looks at the clock when Daddy is gone so I figured it would tell me something, but it tells me nothing!

I wait and wait and wait and still nothing. Mommy doesn't come home. I'm scared. But then I look down and remember that I put on my Superman jammies tonight. Superman isn't scared of nothing, so I'll be scared of nothing too. Superman is a lot like me. He's weird and he can do things, super things that no one knows about, not even my mommy and daddy.

Only Mrs. Jones knows, and she told me that she wouldn't tell a soul. Whatever that means.

I asked Mommy about Mrs. Jones once and she just said Mrs. Jones was a mean old lady, but that can't be right either because she's always super nice to me. I don't think Mrs. Jones would leave a little kid all alone at night when the monsters come out.

I need to find Mrs. Jones.

Lucky for me, she lives at the end of the block. I jump out of bed run to my door taking my teddy with me. I peek out into the hall just in case someone is here, but there's no one. I'm all alone.

I carefully make my way down the stairs. One time I ran too fast, and my feet kept going when my body stopped and I fell down the stairs and it really scared me. Now I'm more careful.

The grippies on the bottom of my footie jammies squeaks on the tile floor between the stairs and the front door. I have to pull three times, with all my strength, before the big lock turns. My heart beats fast in my chest as I turn the knob and open the door. I'm not supposed to go out front without my mom or dad but this is an emergery ... emergerney ... emergency! That's it, emergency.

I hold teddy tight to my body as I run down the street. I want to cry but brave boys don't cry, so the whole way I say over and over, "Superman would be brave. Superman would be brave. Superman would be brave. And I'm just like Superman."

I finally get to the big house at the end of the block with the dark, scary door and I ring the bell. I hear it ring in the house and I shake as I wait and wait. I hope Mrs. Jones is home. If she's not, then I really am all alone.

Lights flick on in the house and then the door pulls open and she's at the door in pink stripped jammies with the Superman logo on them. I knew I could trust her! Maybe she's like Superman too!

"What are you doing here, sweet boy?" she asks.

"Mommy and Daddy left and I'm all alone," I tell her, and I try to suck back the tears. I don't want to cry in front of a girl.

"It's okay," she says as she pushes the door wider. "I've been waiting for you."

"You have?" I ask and I feel my eyes go wide.

All the grownups, except for Ms. Jones, my teacher, and Mrs. Jones, my neighbor, make me feel like I'm a lot of work and they don't always want me around. Could she really have been waiting for me?

"I have," she smiles. "Come on in."

I follow her into the house, and she keeps going into the kitchen.

"Are you hungry?" she asks me. "Maybe a cookie and a glass of milk?"

I nod my head real fast because that sounds awesome. I love cookies and milk. Especially after bedtime! But then I remember that I have to tell Mrs. Jones a secret that might make her upset. I don't want to make her upset because she's a real nice lady.

"Is something on your mind, Timmy?"

"Yeah," I say, kicking the toe of my footies against the tile floor. "But I'm afraid you're not gonna like it."

"Well then, we better get it out really fast so we don't have to worry about it anymore, right?"

"All right."

"What is it?"

"I think my Daddy is going to do something to Ms. Jones," I tell her.

"To Penelope? My granddaughter?"

"Yeah."

"What is he going to do?" she asks.

"I don't know," I admit. "But it's real bad. Mommy was crying when he told her."

"She was?"

"Yeah. Mommy cries a lot when he talks about Ms. Jones. I don't like it."

"He talks about her?" she asks.

I look up at her. She doesn't look mad at all. At least, not at me but I'd bet my baseball cards she's real mad at my daddy.

"He talks about her loads," I tell her, nodding my head. "It makes my mommy real upset."

"I can see why," she says quietly, so quiet I don't think she meant me to hear it.

"Do you?" I ask. "Because I don't get it."

"I'll explain it to you when you're older," she

says with a laugh.

"Okay."

"Do you know where your mommy and daddy went?" she asks me.

"Mommy went after Daddy. She said she was going to fix our family whatever that means."

"And where did your daddy go?"

"I think he went to get Ms. Jones."

"Oh dear," she says.

"I know!" I cry.

"Don't lose it yet," she says. "We still need to be brave."

"Okay," I sniffle.

"Where would your daddy take her?" she asks. "Have you heard him mention anywhere he doesn't normally go lately?"

"He talked about the cabin when he left."

"Good job, Timmy!" she cheers. "Can you tell me where the cabin is?"

"It's in the woods and it's kind of far away," I tell her.

"That's okay," she says. "Everything is going to be okay."

"Really?" I ask. I want to believer her, but I'm still scared.

"Yes," she says with a big smile on her face. "But first, we have to go on an adventure."

30

Taken

HUNTER

6 hours earlier...

"Fuck," I bite out as I look at the red message-not-received notification. I thought it was a fluke, a weird dead zone that had bounced my text message back. I tried again and again, getting nothing but that goddamned try-to-resend icon blinking at me.

I hit Penelope's contact and lift my phone to my ear only to hear *"The number you were trying to reach cannot be connected at this time. If you have received this message in error, please hang up and try again."*

"Fuck!"

"Whoa, there. What's with all of the F-bombs, big man?" Brody asks as he walks up to me.

For a second, I consider telling him that it's none of his fucking business. I don't like to air my fuck ups for the world to see but lying to my best friend would only compound the fuck ups of the day. Even if he's going to beat my ass.

I sigh and run my hand through my hair. The frustrated gesture is one of my only tells. "I fucked up."

"That much is obvious," he replies to my admission. "How so?"

I drop down into my desk chair across from his and pick up my cold by cup of coffee and stare at the contents. "Penelope was dreaming of Sarah's murder."

"What?" he asks quietly as he sits down at his desk across from mine. All traces of humor are wiped clean from his face.

"She's been having visions since before I met her," I admit. "But it's new. She thought the family power skipped her."

"Did it?"

"Apparently not."

"That's what Amanda said as well," he adds. "She was pretty upset that Pen had kept such a big secret from her all these years."

"She didn't know it was her secret to share," I snap.

"I know that," he says, holding his hands up, palms out to me. "And now, so does Amanda. What else is going on?"

"She saw me as the killer."

"Oh shit."

"So the whole time we were together—I was falling for her, *I claimed her*—she was trying to come to terms with falling for a murderer," I tell him. It still fucking stings that she could think so little of me.

"Fuck," he mutters. "That sucks."

"Tell me about it."

"I get that it has to burn knowing she thought you could be capable of something like that. But look at it this way, she cares enough about you that she was trying to come to grips with it and still loves you," he says trying to reassure me. It only reminds me of how badly I've fucked everything up. "What?"

"I lost it when I realized she didn't just think I was Sarah's killer, but her lover as well. And then, you know, Penelope's lover too," I admit. "I said some mean shit that I shouldn't have and kind of broke up with her and then left."

"Wow. There's a lot to unpack there."

"That's not all."

"Tell me you're kidding," he says.

"I wish I were."

"What did you do?" he asks, his voice low with warning.

"Watch it," I warn. "That's my mate."

"Then act like it," he snarls. "What did you do?"

"I broke into her apartment and fucked her and then told her I hated her for how much I wanted her and that I couldn't stay away."

Brody groans and swipes his palm down his face. "You're a fucking moron."

"I know," I admit. "And now she's blocked my number and I can't get a hold of her."

"Okay, two things," he says.

"What's that?" I ask. "And don't call me a moron again—"

"A fucking moron," he interrupts.

"Yes, that. I get it, all right?"

"All right," Brody agrees. "First, you said she thought you were Sarah's lover and killed her."

"Yeah."

"Meaning if we can trust her visions, Sarah was killed by her lover," he explains and my brain spins, jumping to his train of thought.

"Oh shit."

"So my question is, who was Sarah having an affair with?"

"That should be easy enough to find out," I reply. "But getting the evidence to convict is another thing."

"Let's not put the cart before the horse yet," he says. "Now my second thought ..."

"Yes?"

"Penelope agreed to meet Amanda and I for drinks tonight," he says, waving his phone in the air. "You and I go there every now and then, so it's not outside of the realm of possibility that you would show up all on your own."

"You are my favorite friend."

"I think I'm your only friend," he says. "Now, don't fuck it up this time."

I look at my watch. "Looks like I have some time to kill. I better get a warrant for some phone records."

Now...

I take a deep breath and pull my keys from the ignition of my SUV as I spy Penelope's car in the parking lot like a stalker.

I climb from my car and beep the locks before stuffing my keys in my pocket with the phone that Penelope rendered useless sometime today. I'm mad at her for taking away my ability to communicate with her and I'm mad at myself for handling her the way I did. I can't believe I treated her, my mate, so poorly that she wants nothing to do with me. Well, that's about to change.

I pause in front of the door to the bar and wipe my sweaty palms on my jeans. I grab the handle and pull open the door. I spot her immediately. It's like there's a beacon inside her that calls to me. Some unseen force of nature that pulls me into her orbit and I don't even want to fight it. My place is with her.

It seems someone else has been pulled into her orbit as well.

A small growl rumbles up from my chest when I spy the bartender leaning over the bar and smiling at Penelope in a way that leads to late night invitations. I have no one to blame but myself.

A quick look around says that no one but Brody heard me lose my cool over the overly friendly bartender. I make my way through the crowd to where he has Amanda in his arms on the dance floor. I need to talk to him.

"Hey, I haven't seen you here before," a pretty brunette says as she stops my progression. I smile at her and hope that Penelope sees it. A little taste of her own medicine wouldn't hurt her. "Want to dance?" she asks me.

"No," I say gently. "I'm here to meet someone but maybe another time."

"I'm free later," she suggests boldly and before the little witch claimed my heart, I would have taken her up on it. She has a pretty smile and a tight little body, and I can't even summon a dick twitch for all her efforts. And I don't even want to try. "No strings attached. No names either if that's what you're in to."

"Some other time," I say as I gently remove her hand from my arm and make my way to Brody.

"What the fuck was that all about?" Amanda snaps at me. "Brody said you were into Pen and then you make googlie eyes at that hussy over there?"

"Amanda," Brody warns, but it's like a puppy paw. There's no bite to it. In fact, we can both hear the laughter in his voice.

"What the fuck?"

"What the fuck is she offered, and I said no," I growl. "Not that it's any of your business."

"Penelope is my business."

"Penelope is my mate," I warn her. "I'll not have your interference."

"What about hers?" she asks with a devious smile on her face.

"What do you mean?"

"Penelope saw your whole little dance around the slutty brunette," she says with a mean smile on her face. "She left."

"What?" Brody and I say at the same time as we both turn to where she was sitting at the bar. Only her unfinished drink sits on the bar top. Her chair is still swinging back and forth from her hasty exit.

"She's gone," Amanda says. "And a word to the wise, stop playing with my friend. Either you're all in or you're out. No more head games."

"Noted."

"Now go get your mate and make things right," she says.

"Thank you," I tell her softly before I make my way to the back of the bar. "You can run but you can't hide, little rabbit. The big bad wolf will find you anyway."

I follow the scent of her, the one that smells of sunshine, and magic, and now a little whiskey and soda. And something else that intensifies, the closer I get to the restrooms. Something is wrong. Her smell is off, and I know it's because she was sick or in the process of getting sick. But this isn't the everyday human flu; someone drugged my mate.

A roar rumbles up from my chest, low enough for Brody to hear, but not so loud that anyone else in the bar will. He enters the mouth of the hall with Amanda in tow.

"What's wrong?" he asks.

"She's gone. Someone's taken Penelope," I say as I spy her ridiculously huge tote bag dropped by the back door, the contents scattered all over.

"What?" Amanda gasps. "Why? What's happening?"

"Shh, mate," Brody soothes. "We'll find her."

My phone rings and I pull it from my pocket. The ID of the caller surprises me and I slide my finger across the glass to answer. "Buchannon."

"A little birdie told me that my granddaughter

might be missing," the caller says.

"And what little birdie would that be?"

"That doesn't matter yet," she says. "What does matter, is I might know where you can find her."

"I'm listening."

She rattles off an address in the woods and I want to know who is out there, but she doesn't offer any more information. She just offers a terce, "Now go and get our girl." And then she hangs up.

"What was that all about?" Brody asks.

"I think I know where Penelope is," I answer. "And I think I know who killed Sarah Cramer."

"Well, don't keep us waiting."

"It's time to go hunting."

31

Please help me

PENELOPE

My stomach pitches and I blink my eyes. They're blurry and the room is spinning, so I squeeze them closed again. I feel like I'm going to be sick. I try to turn to my side, but I can't. My body won't budge. My eyes fly open and I blink as fast as I can to clear them. It works a little but not enough. The only thing I can tell is that my wrists and ankles are bound.

The bed that I'm lying on depresses next to me and a hand trails down the side of my face.

"Shh," he whispers and I slam my eyes closed again at the sound of his voice. It can't be. This man cannot be the killer of my dreams. "It'll all be all right now. You have given me a merry chase but it's over now and you're mine."

"P-please let me go."

"Now, why would I do that?" he asks. His face begins to come into focus enough that I can see the slimy smile on his face. "I haven't had you yet."

"Why?" I plead. "Why are you doing this? I haven't done anything to you."

"Because I want you," he says as he traces the outline of my breast with the back of his hand. "Because I've wanted you for a long time. Every time, you teased me and then turned down my invitations, it made me so angry."

"But, I didn't—"

"And when I saw you out with that detective," Mr. Simmons says. "I couldn't stand it. I was filled with such a blinding rage. I knew then that you wanted me to be jealous."

"No, not at all," I try to explain but he isn't having any of it.

"So I decided that I would take you and I began to plot and plan how we would spend our time together."

"Please," I beg. "Please let me go."

He just smiles at me. "You're not going anywhere."

Mr. Simmons slowly starts to pluck at the buttons on the front of my blouse.

Tears burn hot down my cheeks. I don't want this. I've never wanted this. I've never flirted with him or teased him. Regardless of what he thinks, I've never promised him anything and I'm not his to take or have. This is nothing but an assault and there's nothing I can do to stop it.

I pray to the goddess to make me forget. Let me peacefully slip from this plane and leave this world and the pain behind. I also ask her to grant peace to my mom and grandma and Mrs. Yee. I don't want them to bear the burden of grief that Mr. Simmons's crimes will leave behind. And last, I want Hunter to find peace as well. He wasn't meant for me, but someone out there will be a beautiful match for him. He's not perfect but he's not evil either.

Mr. Simmoms's phone chimes in his pocket. He drags it out and frowns at the preview. He slides his thumb across the screen and opens his messages. I can't see what it says or who it's from but whatever it is makes him mad.

"Can't I have just one night to do what I fuck-ing want?" he mutters to himself.

I hold my breath hoping whatever it is gives me a reprieve from whatever he's planning to do. I just need him to leave so that I can figure out how to get out of here.

If only my magic worked even a little bit, then I could shake free the bonds that hold me down. But I'd probably blow up the whole building … or nothing would happen at all.

"I'm going to have to go, my darling," he says

gently as he stands. "But don't worry, we'll have more than one night together. I'm not ready to be done with you yet."

Oh god, he's planning on keeping me like this for a while. I have to get out of here.

He stands and makes his way out of the room.

"Please!" I call out. "Don't leave me like this." But he's gone. I hear a door slam and then a car start. He really left me here like this.

I pull at my restraints and they bite into my wrists. Handcuffs. Steel handcuffs scrape and pinch as I pull on them. I'll never get out of them this way.

I close my eyes and try to draw up my magic the way that my mom taught me when I was younger, and just like then, nothing happens. Tears burn my sinuses. I'm just a failure and I'm going to die a failure. The Jones line will die here with me because I'm absolutely useless as a witch and a human.

A noise draws my eyes open. Mrs. Simmons is peaking around the corner. She's here! I'm saved.

"Thank god!" I cry. "Help me!"

"I can't do this," she cries. "I need you to stop whatever hold you have on him."

"I can't! I didn't do anything!" I need her to help me but she won't if she believes that I have a hold over her husband. Hell, I can't even get him to believe I don't want him.

"I know."

Thank god. She's going to help me. I'm going to get out of here alive. "You're going to help me right?" I ask. I need her to find a way to get me out of here.

"I'm going to fix the problem," she says cryptically, and I wonder if maybe the whole family isn't cracked after all.

"Let's just find a way to get these handcuffs off and then I'll just be on my way," I say.

She stares at me as if she doesn't really see me at all. And then, she pulls a gun from her handbag and points it at me.

"No," I cry. "You don't want to do this."

"I don't," she screams. "But you're making me do this. This is all your fault."

"My fault?" I shout. "I haven't done anything wrong."

"It doesn't matter," she says. "I have to end this hold you have on my husband. I have to get him back."

"He's yours. I don't want him."

"But he wants you and that's all that matters."

The bedroom door flies open, and Mr. Simmons appears. *Oh no.*

"What the hell are you doing here, Amy?" he snaps.

"I'm saving our family," she replies. "I have to get rid of her."

Get rid of me? Oh, hell no.

"How about you all just let me go?" I offer. "I'll move, leave town, you'll never see me again."

"I can't do that," Mr. Simmons says. "I need to have her."

"I don't understand," his wife whimpers like a child.

"I know," he says indulgently. "But it's an addiction, a compulsion. I can't stay away."

"And what was Sarah Cramer?" she snaps. "What she an addiction too?"

"No," he laughs. "She was a convenience until she wasn't."

"You didn't need her?" she asks hesitantly.

I feel like I'm watching a tennis match. My blood pressure is rising by the minute and I know that I'm going to die tonight.

"I didn't need her like this."

"Okay."

"Okay?" he asks, hope in his voice.

"Okay," she repeats. "You can have her once and then we'll get rid of her together."

He seems to mull this offer over in his mind and I actually hope he declines because then she'll either kill me outright or I'll have more time to plot my escape. "Deal."

Sonofabitch, I'm going to die in this old hunting cabin tonight. I can't let that happen. But I also can't count on my magic to save me and no one is coming for me. No one knows where I am.

Amanda and Brody probably think I saw Hunter and cut out early. It's not outside the realm of possibility that I would go home to hide out and lick my wounds in private.

Panic rises in my body and I can't stop it. I'm going to be violated by this monster and murdered by another. At least now I know that he was responsible for Sarah's death and my heart swells with sadness that she loved him and he was simply using her.

He steps toward the bed.

I would rather die than let him touch me in front of his wife. I have to do something and yet there's nothing I can do.

My body fills with a growing tide.

My skin shimmers like a mermaid.

And then every window on the cabin blows out.

A wolf howls in the distance.

I swear I see Mom and Grandma in the doorway, but Mr. and Mrs. Simmons don't see them. Grandma winks and then they're gone, but red and blue lights flash on the walls and the sounds of sirens fill the air.

The Simmonses appear to be frozen like statues until the room fills with police and then everything seems to happen all at once.

EPILOGUE

All the time in the world

Two weeks later…

"Can I come in?" Hunter asks as he pushes open the screen door that leads from the backyard of my mom's house into the kitchen. Timmy and I are sitting at the table eating apple slices and drinking glasses of chocolate milk.

"Yes."

He walks in and hands a bouquet of flowers to my mom who smiles, a baseball and glove to Timmy, and a black and white cookie to me. He's been learning how to woo us all. And by the sight of my favorite treat in my hands, he's got my number down.

"I was wondering if I could take you out to a movie tonight after Timmy and I play a bit of catch," he says hesitantly. Watching me, waiting to see if I'll shoot him down.

"I'd like that," I smile at him around a bite of cookie.

"I'm glad," he laughs. "What do you say, Tim?"

"Yes!" he shouts happily. "Let me grab my cap!"

"It's in your backpack!" Mom calls after him.

"Got it!"

Timmy races back to the room with a Yankees cap on his head and then out the back door, making everyone smile at his disappearance. Hunter grabs the gloves and ball and follows him out.

Sometime after the dust settled and the Simmonses were carted off to jail, Timmy admitted to Grandma that they weren't his real parents. Apparently, she had her suspicions all along. Timmy had shown signs of being a magical prodigy and the Simmonses were monsters, but monsters of the very human variety.

After a little digging, it turned out that he was stolen as a baby from a young warlock and his bride in New Jersey after they were murdered in the middle of the night. Mrs. Simmons was desperate to keep her husband in any way she could, so she gave him a son—*someone else's son.*

With no family or coven to claim him, and him being in need of powerful witches who can teach him the ways of our people, it was decided that Grandma would raise him. With the help of Mom,

Mrs. Yee, and myself of course.

I'm not sure how they pulled it off legally and I'm also pretty sure I don't want to know either. In fact, I don't even care. All that matters is, Timmy is safe and I have a feeling deep in my soul that he's right where he belongs.

"You better forgive that man," my mom says, breaking me free from my thoughts.

"We'll see."

"No more 'we'll see'," she says. "Put that man out of his misery. Hasn't he earned your forgiveness yet?"

"Yes," I whisper, knowing that he has.

He said some awful things and I know that he knows he messed up. Since I was rescued, he's done everything in his power to show me how sorry he is and how much he cares for me.

But Mom is right, this unsure look on him is not right. A strong wolf like him should know where he stands. I either need to end things once and for all or let him back into my life, full force.

I know what my choice is.

After a while, Hunter and Timmy come inside. Timmy puts his baseball glove away and comes back to push the stepstool over so he can wash his hands in the kitchen sink. He's settled into a safe and steady routine as part of this family.

Hunter holds out his hand for me to take but the questioning look is still there. It's time to put that look away for good. "Ready?"

I look him in the eye so that he sees I mean more than just dinner and a movie. "I'm ready for anything and everything."

"Thank God."

And then he takes me on a date.

We may not be perfect and we still have a long way to go to figure each other out, but that's the best part about forever. We have all the time in the world.

HEX & CANDY
Gone

I need a cigarette.

I know I shouldn't, but I can't help it. At least I only smoke when I drink. And now that I'm not in college anymore and have grown to be an upstanding citizen, those times are few and far between.

I just don't want Brody to catch me. He's said over and over again that he hates me smoking. Something about my body being a temple and all that shit. I know he's right, but still, I can't help craving the bitter tang of tobacco on my lips and the feel of a cigarette between my fingertips.

Besides, what Brody doesn't know won't kill him. And with the help of some vodka and chewing gum, he won't.

"I need the bad little witches' room," I say with a wink.

Brody drops his mouth to mine in a hard kiss before reluctantly letting me go. God, I love this man. I can't wait to get home and have my wicked way with him. Maybe we can cut this Halloween party short in favor of a private party for two.

"Don't be long," he growls across my lips and I know that he'll be happy to leave early with me.

I hesitate, thinking maybe an orgasm would chase the jumpiness away faster than my need for a cigarette but then again, my wonky synapsis could probably use both.

"I won't."

I make like I'm going to the restroom—everyone knows you have to break the seal sometime so it's a good enough excuse. I bypass the restrooms and head for the door that leads to an alleyway out back. Thankfully, I frequented this bar a time or two while I was finding my college education in the bottom of a pitcher of beer.

The door pushes open with a squeak, and I nervously look around. Thankfully, the sound can't be heard over the raised volume of a full bar of Hallows Eve revelers.

I take a step away from the entrance and the heavy door swings shut with a clang, making a chill run up my spine. I laugh at my silly reaction and head toward my favorite smoke spot.

I take another step—almost there—and slip the pack from my small purse just as my hat is knocked from my head.

"You've been a bad little witch," a voice from the shadows says just before a bag is placed over my head, shutting out the light. He touches my neck with his fingertips, and everything goes dark.

I come awake with a start just as the phone rings. My heart is pounding in my chest and not in the good way. Like it did when Hunter and I played Little Red Ridinghood and the big bad wolf earlier. To say that he liked my costume would be an understatement.

I hear him reach for his phone on the nightstand, stretching to grab it so that he can leave his long, powerful legs tangled with mine.

"Buchannon," I hear him answer, but I already know what the person on the other end of the line is going to say. "Hold tight, Brody. We'll be right there."

"Hunter?" I ask as he sets the phone back on the table. My heart feels like it's beating in my throat.

"Get up, baby," he says gently. "We have to go."

"What's happened?" I ask even though I know in my heart of hearts what he's going to say. And I wish, with every wish I ever had, that I'm wrong even though I know that won't be the case. Because I'm Penelope Jones, wonky witch and newish clairvoyant.

"Amanda's missing," he says, and I know my dream was right.

"She's not missing," I tell him. "She was taken. We need to go."

PLAYLIST

Bad at Love—Halsey

Bad Thing—Machine Gun Kelly & Camillia Cabello

Stay—Kid Laroi & Justin Bieber

Wolves—Selena Gomez &Marshmellow

Arcade—Duncan Lawrence

Hell of a View—Eric Church

ABOUT JENNIFER

Jennifer is the *USA Today Bestselling Author* of the Claire Goodnite series and the Presidential Affair. She is a native of San Diego, California. She credits her love of books and reading to her mother and her knowledge that real heroes do exist to her dad.

Jennifer is a graduate of California State University San Marcos where she studied Criminology and Justice Studies. She is also a member of Alpha Xi Delta.

She currently lives in East Texas with her husband, Sean, and their three children along with an entire menagerie of lovable but sofa eating animals. She can often be found on the soccer or baseball fields, reading, or wondering what the hell her senior citizens have gotten up to now. Jennifer is convinced that if she puts her Apple Watch on one of the dogs, she might finally make her step goals.

She loves a great romance, an alpha hero, and lots and lots of laughter.

STALK HER

www.facebook.com/jenniferrebeccaauthor
www.instagram.com/jenniferrebeccaauthor
www.tiktok.com/jenniferrebeccaauthor
www.twitter.com/jennirlreads
www.pinterest.com/jennirlreads

And join in the fun with the Dangerous Dames:
www.facebook.com/groups/JRdangerousdames

ALSO BY JENNIFER

The Funerals and Obituaries

Dead and Buried

Dead and Gone

Dead and Deceived

Dead and Wed

I met a Girl

Murder on Ice

Attack Zone

Layback

The Claire Goodnite Series

Tell Me a Story

Tuck Me in Tight

Say a Sweet Prayer

Kiss Me Goodnight

The Liam Goodnight Series

Hush Little Baby

Don't Say a Word

The Presidential Affair

The Senator's Secret

Caught by the Chief of Staff

The Press Secretary's Passion

The Vice President's Mistress

The Southern Heartbeats
Stand
Whiskey Lullaby
Joy
Mercy
Just a Dream
Church Bells

Standalones
Trap: A Salvation Society Novel
Dark Horse: A Driven World Novel
Counterplay

With Alyssa Kale
Ready to Run

Accidental Hex
Birthday Hex
Hex and Candy
Love Hex Magic

The Wildflowers
Wildflower
Wild Heart
Wild Child
Wild Card